KETTLE LANE

THE ROOKERY BOOK ONE

B G DENVIL

Cover design by
It's A Wrap

BY BARBARA GASKELL DENVIL

The Rookery

KETTLE LANE

THE PIDDLETON CURSE

HOBB'S HENGE

BANNISTER'S MUSTER

(A MIDDLE GRADE TIME TRAVEL ADVENTURE)

SNAP

SNAKES & LADDERS

BLIND MAN'S BUFF

DOMINOES

LEAPFROG

HIDE & SEEK

HOPSCOTCH

There are other books written under my full name, Barbara Gaskell Denvil— but these are not Cosy, and contain elements of violence, swearing and sexual content.

You can find them on my website at barbaragaskelldenvil.com

For my daughter Gill, who came up with the idea and designed my beautiful covers.

CHAPTER ONE

Brimming with a smile as wide as a cucumber, and all her dimples cuddling each other, Alice told her daughter, "Well, Rosie, it has happened at last. The Rookery finally has a vacancy."

Dropping the scrubbing brush in surprise, Rosie stared back at her mother. "How? No one ever dies. No one ever leaves. Has they built another room on the back or something?"

Alice shook her bedraggled black curls, her smile still wide enough to show off her vacant gums. "No, no, stupid child. At long, long last, Whistle Hobb has left us."

"Wow!" Rosie gasped. "Did you upset him? Or has he discovered a long-lost daughter to go and stay with?"

"Whistle Hobb has finally died," Alice announced, her smile now a sudden frown. "Utterly dead. Not a flutter of breath remains. And in fact," and here she lowered her voice to a conspiratorial whisper, "there are signs he may have been murdered. Cursed perhaps. Or something even more dramatic."

"What's more dramatic than murder?" Rosie ignored the scrubbing brush she had dropped and walked towards one of the many tiny rickety staircases. One foot to the first step, she turned.

"Honestly, Mother, Whistle was probably the most powerful wizard in this house. Who had the capability of killing such a man?"

"You just go and clean up," Alice said, flopping onto the nearest stool. "His rooms are sure to be a horrible mess, and I can't advertise the vacancy while his room's still a dump."

Rosie sighed and continued up the creaking steps. She was half way up when her mother yelled, "By the way. The body's still in there. You'll have to think of somewhere to put it."

"In a cupboard perhaps? Or the sewerage heap?" Stopping mid creak, Rosie gulped. "I can hardly bundle him off to church for a respectable burial. They'll guess. He's not exactly respectable, is he!"

"Perhaps a pyre in the back garden. Or one of those crossroads affairs."

Rosie didn't answer, but plodded along the small corridor to the two rooms previously, and apparently still, occupied by one of her favourite inmates. She stifled her increasing nausea. Rosie had liked Whistle rather a lot, she'd also admired him, being such a powerful and humorous wizard. Helpful too. Her own magical powers were shamefully small, but Whistle had taught her a thing or five.

The bedchamber contained a bed somewhere, but it took Rosie sometime to find it. The clutter of papers, scrolls, papyrus, rice paper and parchment, many of these documents floated and scrambled to arrive on the top of the piles, and generally called for attention. This made it a little difficult to actually collect them, let alone prioritise them. Some, Rosie decided, might be important or even give clues as to who, how and why the murder had taken place.

"Me, I'm important." One parchment scroll was flapping in her face. She felt rather rude, pushing it away, but discovering roughly twenty thousand different papers of different kinds, she dismissed the idea of reading them all.

"But I am worth reading," the unrolling scroll insisted, flicking its corner into Rosie's face.

"You've put me off," she replied firmly. "You scratched me."

"Then read me instead," whined a small piece of rice paper containing a long inky list. "I'm only little. You could read me in just a moment or two."

"I can't read all of you," Rosie complained. "Too many."

"The others," said a loud and deep voice, "are of no importance whatsoever. Just read me."

"They're all pathetic," squeaked a folded parchment. "But me, I'm a big favourite. Master Whistle loved me dearly."

"So, did any of you," Rosie shouted over the clamour, "see what happened to Whistle? Or see who came into his rooms?"

There was a rather inane flapping of disappointment. "No," said one sadly. "Master Hobb lies in the other room. He didn't come to bed last night."

"And no one visited," said a large scroll. "At least, no one came into this room."

Rosie sniffed. "Not even the maid?"

"'Tis usually you is the maid," an illuminated manuscript pointed out, making a dramatic twist mid air. "And dear Master Hobb is lying in the other room. His study, he called it."

"So did you hear anything odd?" asked Rosie, stopping suddenly. "Honestly, you could at least tidy yourselves a bit."

"We don't know who goes with what," a few voices chimed together. "And we all have different subjects so how can we make one pile?"

"Because," said Rosie, horrified, "it will take me all day."

"Oh, bother," muttered a small paperback from the future.

CHAPTER TWO

W histle Hobb's study was an extension of the bedchamber, for he slept rarely and spent most of his two hundred and sixteen years investigating, reading and inventing. Somewhere under the thousands of papers next door, there had surely been a bed, presumably with blankets and pillows, a chamber pot, and a chest for clothes, money and other essentials. Beneath the endless papers, no bed had been visible, but it surely existed.

The second room presented a sadly different drama. The body of a small man lay prone on the floorboards. Whistle wore a costume very untypical for the year 1484, which was the date of his death. The eighteenth of April, to be exact. But instead of the expected doublet and hose, he was wearing a pair of brightly striped pantaloons, a green satin shirt and a navy-blue duffle coat. His feet, however, were bare, and since he was lying flat on his face, the bizarre tattoo of a crow was visible on both soles of his feet. These crows had invariably whistled when Master Hobb walked around. But they whistled no longer and appeared deeply dejected.

His hair, quite white but rather bushy, covered the back of his head, along with a huge area of dried blood. There was more. Blood splatters decorated the entire room, and even the old beamed ceiling was marked with visible red spots. One of the beams appeared virtually repainted, and lying separate on the floor, Whistle's black velvet wizard's cape kept flapping in panic.

Since the only window was particularly minute with tiny green glass mullions, Rosie had lit a candle. The cape kept blowing it out. She wondered if Whistle would manage to come back as a ghost and haunt the place, giving clues as to his unexpected ending. Master Hobb wasn't just some back-street necromancer. He was, had been, a mighty powerful sorcerer. To imagine anyone strong enough to slaughter him was a terrifying puzzle.

With the small flash of one index finger, Rosie turned him over. His face had been smashed. This had been a tortuously brutal crime, and Rosie ran from the room.

"I'll clean up later," she told her mother. "But I'll need help."

"Don't leave it too long. Perhaps get some of the crows in," Alice suggested. She was reading *Ye Olde Recipe for the Best Pottage and Pastry*, but since Rosie knew quite well her mother usually cooked by magic and had probably never lifted a saucepan in her life, she was perfectly sure the old woman was simply pretending to be busy so she wouldn't have to offer help herself.

"But I am getting quite a headache and must go back to bed. Besides, I have to word the advertisement for the new resident to take up the vacancy. Obviously, I can't just write '*Comfy cosy place available for an aging witch or wizard'.* We'd all be carried off to Newgate."

"And where are you going to hang this notice then?"

Alice considered the matter. "One on the outside of the old Guildhall, and I'll stick another on the yew tree."

"What happens if a normal human unenchanted soul turns up?"

"I shall think about it," said Alice. The book on her lap (one of William Caxton's early printings) was upside down, but this was often her preferred habit. "In the meantime, ask silly little Lemony

Limehouse to help with the cleaning, and perhaps old Boris Barnacle will help with the heavy lifting. He can use all ten fingers, you know."

"I can lift poor Whistle using just two," Rosie said with a superior shrug. "But Boris might be useful with a wet cloth. Did you see that place? It's a massacre."

"I suppose," her mother said after a short pause, "we should make some attempt to find out who did it." She copied Rosie's shrug. "I shan't miss the wretched old show-off, of course, but we can't risk having a killer on the premises."

"I'd already decided on that," Rosie said, small voiced. "But I need help with that too, and it won't be Boris or Lemony I'll ask."

"Percy Rotten? The Butterfield woman? Or nice little Harry Flash?"

"None of them," answered Rosie. "You just get on with your advert offering a double room vacancy on The Rookery premises for old folk in need of care. Specialising in–?"

"The Rookery," Alice said with pride, "is not just for old folk who can't be bothered looking after themselves. This is a House of Care specialising in wiccan folk. We are, in case you have forgotten, a high quality wiccary. And since none of these medieval nitwits know what that means, they cannot apply."

"Do what you like," sniffed Rosie. "I'm off to find my wiccan accomplice. Not, not you, mother. You're only a fifty."

"No need to bring that up." Alice returned to her upside-down book, but muttered, "Which is all you are yourself, my girl."

"I'm not ashamed of it," Rosie said. "But I'm hoping to team up with an eighty-five." Scurrying out, she at least thanked her lucky stars, of which she only had a couple and they rarely came out, that her mother seemed in a good mood for once. Poor Whistle's death evidently pleased some, but half the old house hardly knew him, for Whistle had kept himself to himself for many long years. He was far too busy making his own spells and inventions, and invented his own much nicer food as well.

Her mother's watery gunge was not loved by many but most simply enjoyed meeting and chatting over the long dining table.

Rosie was deeply sorry she could never again privately meet and chat with Whistle.

CHAPTER THREE

P eg lived in one of the attics, not that she climbed all those stairs. She used the window. Having a rather poor memory, sometimes she forgot to open the window first, but this usually made little difference, apart from a collection of multi-coloured bruises over her forehead.

She did, however, open the door when someone knocked. "Ah, dear little Rosie Scaramouch. What a surprise." And then closed the door in Rosie's face.

"I haven't come in yet," Rosie called through the keyhole. Then, since Peg already knew who she was, Rosie walked through the closed door and smiled. "I just wanted to discuss something," she said, sitting on the unmade bed. "I have a proposition."

"My husband propositioned me once," Peg remembered, with a faraway smile. "But that was a very long time ago. He went off to discover the New World ninety-eight years gone, he hasn't come back yet."

"My proposition is a little different," Rosie admitted. "Did you know that Whistle Hobb was murdered last night? I want you to help me find out who did it. No one else seems much interested, but anyone powerful enough to smash the head of a ninety, is a very dangerous person."

"A ninety? Yes, A ninety-two, if he told me the truth. But, my dear, I am only an eighty-five."

"I'm a fifty, like my mother," Rosie mumbled with a faint blush. "But together we'd make a hundred and thirty-five. Now that's a reasonable power-house, don't you agree? Poor Whistle. I think we should."

With a brief fiddle of her fingers, having momentarily forgotten the right order, Peg made the bed and changed her clothes. "Ping Pong, now we'll be gone," she said loudly, flicking fingers on both hands, and immediately they both appeared in the kitchen.

Alice looked up and jerked awake. "I wish you wouldn't do that," she objected. "It's most disconcerting. Besides, you usually use the window."

Peg shook her head. "It's raining."

"Bother." Alice closed her eyes again.

"Which means," Rosie interrupted her, "we can't bury poor Whistle in the back yard yet. Can't light a fire, the ground will be as sloshy as your pottage."

Her mother became steel-eyed and opened her mouth to shout, but this time Peg interrupted. "Thing is, my dear," she said, discovering another stool under the table and sitting down with a bump, "our dear Whistle was a mixed bunch of daffodils. A little know-it-all, which annoyed some. But that was just because he really did know-it-all. He was a ninety-two. Now who, magical or human, is clever enough to kill a ninety-two? So," and her smile grew as she clasped her thin fingered hands in her emerald velvet lap, "I suggest, my dear Alice, it is you who should clean up, since you are our much appreciated hostess, and do sort poor Whistle's funeral too. In the meantime, with a little help from our friends, Rosie and I will solve this mystery."

Alice kept glaring, though saying nothing which might come back against her in the future. Peg, after all, was probably now the strongest witch in the entire house, and it would be most unwise to antagonise her. Although she had a poor memory and was known as completely scatty, Peg was a proven wonder house of oddities. So Alice stood, the glare fixed, and walked to the door. Here, she rang the large brass bell hanging high at the door jamb, and waited for some of her more helpful inmates to come rushing to see what she wanted.

The Rookery was an old cottage, thatched in large parts, tin roofed in patches, and covered by slate on the rest. Although from the outside the cottage appeared to contain perhaps thirty small rooms or less, in fact, there were forty very large rooms tucked inside. There was a kitchen naturally, a spacious meeting hall with a huge inglenook large enough for Cinderella, and the garden outside which was huge and ran almost the length of Kettle Lane. The house itself was called The Rookery, but the actual rookery surrounded the house. There were nests for a hundred crows or more. Most of the time there were indeed a hundred crows or more. Though some of them kept to themselves and minded their own business, there were one or two who expected to have regular conversations with the witches. And besides, their own business often coincided.

Amongst the rooms within The Rookery, lived a large community of aged witches and wizards, all of whom had far more need to be looked after than any wish to do it for themselves. Yes, you could summon up a reasonable dinner with a click of experienced fingers, but that didn't mean to say it always turned out in a good state. The roast lamb could be burnt. The pork chops could be underdone. And worst of all, the rainbow trout, instead of being stuffed with sage and onion could suddenly arrive stuffed with hollyhocks and rhubarb.

Not that Alice's cooking was trouble free, frequently it was either entirely lacking in taste, or tasted of toe nail clippings and sardine scales, but at least all the inhabitants could then blame Alice and not themselves.

The wiccan inmates were all content to live in one or two rooms each, and be thoroughly looked after. Most were graded a little above sixty, since this was considered the average in magical power. But some, like Peg, were a good deal stronger, even if they were forgetful and apt to say their spells muddled.

As a few of the more obediently helpful inmates came running or appearing to see what Alice wanted, both Peg and Rosie left the kitchen and went quickly into the communal salon. It was more spacious and comfortable than the others. But it was distinctly chilly and the fireplace was empty even of a few hot sooty ashes. It was officially spring, and once spring had sprung, whatever the weather actually decided to do with itself, no fire was lit and the common salon remained hot or cold depending on the sun, or lack of it, through the windows. There were chairs and rugs and even a mottled mirror on one wall, but this did not mean the room was cosy. Indeed, it was distinctly chilly.

"Now," Peg said, clapping her wizened hands, "if we're going to do this, let's get started. Are we looking for a human or a wizard?"

"Everyone. Everything," Rosie answered, rubbing her hands together. She had often attempted magical self-warming over the years, but so far had never succeeded. Now the rain was hurtling against the windows, and Rosie stared out with irritation. "I suppose we will just have to talk indoors," she said. "I doubt you have the power to stop the rain?"

Peg shook her matted white topknot. "No, dear. I don't think even Whistle Hob could do that. But I could fly us into the village so quickly that we wouldn't get wet."

Looking from her ice-tipped fingers to the dark hanging shadows, Rosie nodded with delight. "Brilliant idea".

Not so large but a good deal warmer, the Juggler and Goat was Little Piddleton's one and only tavern, and with a whoosh unseen by the locals since everyone was indoors avoiding the rain, Peg and Rosie arrived at the front door and hurried inside. Sitting at a vacant table amongst the other vacant tables, they felt safe from eavesdroppers. Then, over large pewter tankers of strong ale, Rosie and Peg settled to discuss their plans.

"Well," Peg announced, "The future begins now, my dear," and she buried her nose in her cup.

"Humph," said Rosie. "This may mean just a bit of plain investigation with a bit of magic mixed in. I like the sound of that. But where do we start?"

Peg was snuffling into her ale. "Trouble is," she said with a sniff, "I do tend to get my magic back to front these days. You just have to put up with some spells going topsy-turvy. Upside down. Under the eiderdown. And don't forget, my dear, I am quite an old lady now. Yesterday I celebrated, rather privately, my two hundredth and one years. So not too much exercise please."

"Not even a quick whizz around on the broomstick at night?" Rosie asked.

"Oh, goodness gracious me," scoffed Peg. "I'm not interested in anything that old-fashioned. If I wish to exercise, rare as that is, I shall ride one of the bats. I'm very friendly with most of the bats, you know. After all, I live in the attic, and they live in the beams or the broken chimney. So we know each other quite well."

"I can't imagine the bats are going to help us very much in this sort of situation," Rosie said. "What can such a little furry thing do? I don't think even the crows will be able to help. Besides the crows are nesting and tending their eggs. April is baby time. Perhaps the bats are having their babies now too."

Sniffing down her nose, which was long with just a tiny twist on the end, was an easy expression for Peg. "Stuff and beetle-brained hog's tails," she said. "Now, let's get to work. Actually, we have three possible categories of criminal to investigate. There's the wizard – be he necromancer, small-time magician, or powerful sorcerer. There's also the human species. Not usually very interesting, but they can do a lot of damage when they try. And not to be forgotten – are the ghosts."

"Oh bother," Rosie sighed. "I had forgotten them."

"I think I shall change to wine," Peg smiled, which puzzled Rosie since this had nothing to do with what they had been talking about.

"Wine for what?"

"For me to drink, silly." Peg tapped her fingers on the table top, and immediately the landlord appeared, looking somewhat startled.

"Did you call, mistress?" he asked, voice flustered. "Not quite sure how I got here. I were just doing the washing up."

"We need two nice big cups of best Burgundy," Peg grinned. "And no doubt when you get back to your bucket, you'll discover all the cups and platters clean as a duckling feather." She looked up at Rosie across the tiny wooden table and its beer stains and ale puddles. "A little lubrication, my dear, is the trick that makes all magic work better. Now – what were we saying?"

"Ghosts," Rosie reminded her once the landlord had gone. "Now I have to admit, I've never seen one. Are you sure we have to consider them?"

"One day maybe I will introduce you to some of mine," Peg told her. "A couple are quite sweet, but there's one that can be rather brackish. In the meantime, we should compare notes. Any wizards you don't trust? Although this was a brutal crime, a witch might be just as capable."

The tavern was small and dark, but since it was raining, the barman had lit a couple of candles to make it all seem more welcoming. The rain seeped under the door and was creating an elongated stream, urged on by the draught. The main room wasn't full, but Little Piddleton was a small village, and on a rainy day few people felt the need to rush outside, even those from The Rookery. A few sat with their noses in their cups. Since Rosie and Peg sat in one of the darker corners, they could not be overheard, but several of the men peeped over their tankards to see the rare arrival of females, one old, wizened, liver-spotted, small and quite ravishingly unattractive. The other female, however, was young and extremely pretty. Girl and Granny, the men assumed, as Rosie sipped her wine, and Peg quickly drained her cup.

As Peg waved imperiously for a refill, Rosie said, "That's actually quite easy. Starting with the wizards – first, there's my father. Dearest Daddy. He's only a twenty, he's awfully sweet, but he likes sitting out with the crows, or if it's raining, he sits in the chicken shed. He can manage a few things, but not much. As a twenty, he can hardly do up his doublet."

"Not on my list, then."

"Number two, little Boris Barnacle. He's a bit of a tadpole, and has some bodily strength but not much else. He's a twenty-four. He likes pretending he could be a wrestler when they get invented."

Peg drained her cup a second time. The barman was watching now so she didn't have to wave. Recognising a good customer with a usefully eager appetite for booze, he came over at once with the jug.

"Number three, Toby Tuckleberry, is a sixty, and number four, Mandrake Karp, is a seventy-one. Toby's nice but Mandrake is an arrogant pig. Whereas my number five, Montague – well," she lowered her voice, "I admit I rather like him. And he's a seventy-eight."

Now Peg was draining another cupful. "Tell me about old Emmeline Brimstone. I can't stand the woman. She's capable of murderous coshing, I'd wager. She definitely tried to kill me off once. Poison. Probably jealous. Not that I ever talk to her."

Just a little confused once again, Rosie said, "But I like her. She conjured up chocolate smarties for me, and since chocolate hasn't been discovered yet, I was quite impressed."

"Woman's never given me anything except once she left a melting mess of dark brown poisonous stuff on my pillow, which even my magic couldn't clean up and I had to use a real cloth to clean it. Took ages, and smelled disgusting."

"I think," Rosie was cautious, "that might have been a gift of chocolate."

"Enough." Peg slurped her last dregs of wine, held up one hand and stood abruptly with a slight quiver of one knee. "Poison doesn't count as a gift."

With a hurried slurp of her own remaining cup of wine, Rosie looked up. "Where are you going?"

"This is getting us nowhere. We need to watch and wait. In the meantime, it's stopped raining so we ought to be getting home."

"How do you know it's stopped raining?" enquired Rosie, staring at the encroaching river beneath the closed door.

"Oh, dear, don't be silly," Peg croaked, wrapped her scarf around her neck a little too tightly. "Kindly remember I'm an eighty-five. Indeed, I'm probably an eighty-six by now."

There seemed little point in arguing, so Rosie slapped down the required coins on the table, nodded to the barman, and followed Peg outside. She had been correct, of course, the rain had stopped. It was chilly for a spring evening, but well wrapped, both women trotted out and headed for the village outskirts and the fork in the road which led to Kettle Lane.

Peg was in the middle of talking when she disappeared. "Oh dear, dear, dear," she was saying, "the wind is growing str-" and with a shudder, she was gone.

Staring in agitation, Rosie stood and called. She began to wonder what had happened and made a mental list as she always did. "One, she could have been swept off her feet by the wind. Two, she could have decided to fly herself home and forgot to take me with her. Three, she could have been abducted by wicked magicians, such as the one who killed Whistle. Four, the crows? No, surely not the crows. I would have noticed."

Amidst the bluster and howl of the gale, Peg abruptly reappeared. She was obviously disconcerted and apologised as she grabbed her scarf and her cloak collar, pulled her hat over her ears and held onto the feather, while wiping her nose on the back of her other hand.

"What happened?"

"Dear, oh dear," Peg sniffed. "That was a mess. The wind, you know. Most uncomfortable. So I decided no one was about to see us, and I'd fly us both home."

"So what happened?"

"My fingers got mixed up," Peg confessed. "A touch of arthritis, you see. I ended up in Mongolia. The Gobi Desert. I don't recommend it, dear. Not a nice place at all at this time in history. Strange animals and things with lumps on their backs, and people playing with eagles. Most unpleasant. And deserts are supposed to be hot, you know. At least, that's what I read in *Ye Olde Lonely Planet*. But the Gobi was freezing. Haunted too."

"I thought you liked ghosts?"

"Only when they speak English and don't stare from the shadows."

Trudging the last few steps home, neither spoke. Nor did either attempt to fly back home. One mistake was enough. Clutching cloaks and hats, they stumbled over wet cobbles and finally arrived within sight of the old cottage, and were met, as usual, by the chattering and squawking of the crows. Some were comparing eggs and squabbling over who had the prettiest.

But then Peg turned to ask Rosie whether she wished to walk in the front door, or fly straight up to Peg's bedchamber window, when the next inconvenient loss became obvious.

For now, it was Rosie who had disappeared.

CHAPTER FOUR

Scrabbling with fingers and thumbs, Peg sailed through the kitchen window of The Rookery and stared belligerently at Alice. "Quick, quick," she demanded. "What's the spell for getting someone back without knowing where they are? I've forgotten."

"I have no idea. You're supposed to be the eighty-five." Alice tried to look haughty. Then she got the point. "Where's my Rosie?"

"Disappeared," said Peg, both thumbs in a tangle.

Alice rushed immediately to the kitchen bell and rang it over so many times she gave herself a headache. "My little girl," she shrieked. "Come find my Rosie."

Jumbling and flapping, the entire Rookery flew, ran, slid the balustrade, jumped and generally pushed downstairs, cloaks tangled together and everyone shouting at the same time.

"Our little Rosie?" yelled Harry Flash. "Who took her?"

Emmeline appeared through the window. "My favourite little fifty," she wailed. "How did she disappear?"

"And where did she go?" Marmaduke demanded.

Peg, despite the humped shoulders and crooked back, hopped onto the kitchen table and gazed down at the entire collection of The Rookery inhabitants. "You lot just listen to me," she waved a carving knife discovered on the table. "She may not have the strongest magic amongst us, but she's the nicest. So get moving. We need to find her now."

"You lost her?" Marmaduke frowned.

"Just be careful," Peg glared. "I'm stronger than you, twiddle-top. Rosie was with me when she just upped and blinked out." She refrained from admitting her own brief visit to the Gobi Desert. "And we have a murderer in our midst. We need to find Rosie and double quick, before she's the second sacrifice."

"Whistle Hobb was no sacrifice," muttered Percy, the only wizard remaining of the Swamp family. "Rotten old show-off, he was. I reckon someone just got fed-up with his show-off clothes and show-off habits."

Toby looked up. "So you did it? Was that a confession?"

"Now, now, gentlemen," Alice insisted. "It's Rosie we're looking for. I warn you all – no Rosie – no Rookery. I shall close it down."

Only a moment's silence followed before everyone spoke again. Maggs sat on the floor in one corner and fumbled into her collar, trying to trace any disappearance over the past five hours. Two of the witches galloped into the back garden to find sufficient peace and air for their spells to work.

Dandy Duckett crawled under the kitchen table and began to count. "One, two, three, four, someone's knocking on the door. Five, six, seven, eight, it's already getting late. Nine, ten, eleven, twelve—"

Everybody had their own individual systems.

Leaning almost casually against the door jam, Marmaduke was muttering to himself, and at his feet, crouched and muttering a little louder, Butterfield tapped her fingers on her knees.

Marching up and down Alice was quietly sniffing as the push and shove of others still raced up and down the stairs, until finally Cabbage the owl, who nested in the thatch during the day, poked her head in the back window, wondering what was going on. Peg noticed her at once.

"Cabbage, dear, sorry about the horrid noise. Can't be helped, I'm afraid. Have you seen Rosie?"

"Quite often," said the owl, turning her head in something resembling a complete circle. "Why? Has she changed?"

"Of course not," Peg said, somewhat annoyed. "But she's disappeared." And then she thought of something else. "Last night, Cabbage, you were up and about, I'm sure. What happened at Whistle Hobb's window? Did anyone fly in? Did you hear anything strange?"

"Toowit," Cabbage decided. "Saw nothing. Heard plenty."

Peg smiled, and waited, then objected, "Don't just sit there. Tell me what you heard."

"You woke me from a deep sleep," Cabbage pointed out. "Most insensitive. But I shall answer you briefly. I heard a lot of noise. Does that explain enough?"

Peg heaved a sigh. "No, Cabbage. I need details."

"I heard a small black rat under a bush," the owl remembered, scratching beneath one wing. "I swooped down to catch it, but a little stray cat dashed out and got it before I did. I heard the kitten meow. That's what they do, you know. I considered swooping down and taking the kitten too, and would have had two meals in one swoop. But I couldn't be bothered. Then I heard thunder. I was pleased. I quite like the rain. Most refreshing."

Managing to hold off the temptation to scream, Peg said softly, "Not all that, Cabbage, dear. I only need to know what you heard coming from Whistle's room."

"Absolutely nothing, of course, as usual," said the owl, and with a bob of irritation, she flew back up to her bed in the thatch.

"Oh, piffle and swish," Peg muttered, stamping one pointed boot on top of the kitchen table, "I call this a wonky-witted pile of pink pendulums. Nothing makes any sense."

And then there was suddenly a very non-magical knock, imperious and demanding, on the front door. "Oh, bother, now what?" demanded Alice, and stalked off to answer.

The man waiting there was unmistakably human. "I believe I've met you once before, madam," he said, grey eyes penetrating. "I am Dickon Wald, the assistant sheriff for Wiltshire. And I was just passing, you see, when I saw this young lady and wondered if she needed help. I asked her. But she simply smiled and told me she couldn't remember what she needed so couldn't ask. But I can't believe she should stay where she is."

Alice looked past him and squeaked.

On the wide doorstep lay Rosie, flat on her back with both hands crossed over her chest as though in holy resignation, her eyes wide and bright while gazing up past the sheriff at the passing clouds. "Oh my goodness, Rosie, darling," Alice squealed and pushing the young man out of her path, she knelt by her daughter and took one of her hands. "My dearest beloved," she said, using words she had never before used to her daughter since Rosie turned three. "Tell me, beloved, are you feeling alright? And where the blazes did you go?"

Peg stared. This was definitely an exaggeration, since usually Alice called her daughter a useless and lazy little brat.

Alice then abruptly realised something else, for Rosie no longer wore the clothes she had worn that morning. Indeed, she now wore clothes she had never owned.

Everyone stared. From the doorstep, Rosie smiled back. She wore a high waisted gown of heavy damask in purples and blues, with a deep green silk shift beneath. Her hair had been styled into elaborate long curls with a plethora of ruby and pearl pins, which all seemed authentic, and her feet were clasped into tiny green leather booties over fine black silk stockings.

Such clothes were worn by royalty and the very rich, but they were not worn by Alice's daughter, who spent most of her life sweeping floors, making beds, wiping up messes and scrubbing tables. Nor was this a costume any sensible witch bothered to climb into, since they were neither young nor pretty, nor did they often go out to the city. Country maidens wore rubbish. Cheaper and easier and didn't need washing too often.

But when Marmaduke marched outside to see what was going on, he seemed entirely overcome and stood for some minutes with his mouth open. The sheriff's assistant, meanwhile, marched indoors and looked around with interest. "There's been another problem, I'm afraid," he said, not looking in the least afraid of anything. "Several of your neighbours have complained about a recent smell. Decay, death and debauchery, I've been told. So I shall have to investigate."

Peg was already outside, bending over Rosie. "What were you doing?" she demanded. "And where on earth did you get those clothes?"

"Hello, lady," smiled Rosie. "You have a funny nose. Clothes? Don't you like them? I think somebody gave them to me."

"Can you stand up?" Marmaduke peered down, and snapped his mouth shut.

"Why should I?" asked Rosie. "I'm quite comfy down here. Have I been here long?"

"Not on the doorstep," said Peg with a twitch of her insulted nose.

Having pushed inside after the unexpected and unwanted human, Alice clenched her hands. "Master Sheriff," she said with an extremely false smile, "this house belongs to me, and I care for twenty aged and infirm poor dears, who have neither the coin nor the ability to look after themselves. You have no right to march in here and disturb them."

"Even those lying on your doorstep in clothes that the queen might not be able to afford?"

"The dear queen died a month ago," Alice said with careful patience. "Or didn't you know such an important tragedy had occurred? Perhaps you're only interested in funny smells."

With reluctance, Rosie hauled herself into a sitting position, her back resting against the open door. "What a strange old place," she said. "But it looks – just faintly – familiar. How do you do, madam? Do you live here?"

Peg managed to bend over far enough to plop herself down on the doorstep beside Rosie. "Your name, girl?" she insisted. "Come on, tell me."

The doorstep was not the cleanest in the country. The wide stone slabs were ingrained with moss, damp grit, crawling beetles, and a number of muddy footsteps. Rosie appeared entirely unconcerned. "My name?" she smiled. "I can't really remember. It's an interesting question. Now, I wonder, did I ever have a name? Peggy, perhaps? I seem to remember a Peggy."

"That's me."

"Really? How quaint," Rosie said. "Perhaps we could share."

"I'll give you three names," Peg frowned. "You pick the right one. Ready? Alice. Rosie. Butterfield." She paused. "Go on, then. Pick one."

The oddly dressed girl on the doorstep continued to smile, "I really like the name Butterfield," she said. "But it's Alice, isn't it? I'm quite sure now. My name's Alice."

"Oh, I give up." Peg sniffed, climbed up and walked back indoors. Finding Alice, she sniffed again. "Your idiot girl has been worked over."

Having discovered the back window in the kitchen, which, although mullioned, gave a wide view of the grounds in The Rookery's rear, the sheriff's assistant had gone rigid. He gazed out at the destruction of an old man lying on the grass, seemingly dressed with similar eccentricity to the girl on the front doorstep, but unlike the girl on the front doorstep, this body was quite dead.

"His head," Dickon said with faint nausea, "has been smashed in with a force akin to a battering ram. Who is that person? What happened to him?"

Having now reappeared, Peg sighed. "We know who he is, poor Whistle. Used to live here. A friend to us all. The clothes were his own choice. He was a little odd, you know. Anyway, not being a good Christian, we had no intention of taking him to the local church for burial. But who did this? We've no idea. Somewhat upsetting."

"You intended burying this poor man in your own back garden?"

Alice pushed in. "Why not?" she demanded with strident insistence. "It's what he would have liked. But discovering the killer is uppermost. Now, since you're a sheriff, why don't you give a suggestion?"

Rosie had finally floated from the doorstep and now stood beside her mother. "Hello," she said with a vague friendliness. "Who are you? Are you another Butterfield?"

"We shall all be dragged off to Bedlam within the hour," muttered Montague on his way up the stairs. "Call me for supper."

Alice was trying to hug Rosie, but Rosie was trying very hard to extricate herself. Neither took much notice of the human, but Peg managed to interrupt, saying, "You can help if you like, So, who slaughtered Whistle Hobb? He was clever, rather old, could be bossy, but was never mean, and couldn't have been killed by any of our residents. They're all far too old."

Dickon looked down on her since he was roughly double her height. "I have every intention of investigating the matter," he said, frowning. "You can start by burying the poor old gentleman, if you're sure he wouldn't want a Christian ceremony." He glanced over his shoulder at Rosie, who smiled back. "Perhaps I could attend the burial and say a few words. Ashes to ashes and so forth. I mean, I'm not a priest, but I do know what to say."

"Wonderful," Peg glowed, clapping her hands. "Bless you, or whatever it is they say. We might do it tomorrow morning."

But Dickon shook his head. "Your neighbours have complained of the stench," he pointed out, with another quick smile over his shoulder at Rosie. "I believe you should do it now. I shall give you a hand."

Everyone stared back, wondering how they could get out of it.

But again, Peg spoke. "Spades," she said softly, "are stacked in the old shed outside. Our gardener Dipper will help, naturally. And then we can bury this poor soul in peace."

"I take it," continued the sheriff's assistant, "no last rights were spoken. In these shocking cases of illegal killing, there's no time to call a priest. So he will, sad wretch, be fated to walk forever in purgatory."

"Oh, I doubt that," Peg grinned. "I expect he'll go somewhere entirely different. But he won't object."

Looking around, puzzled but seemingly searching for truth, Rosie stared from toes to ceiling and window to door. "I have an idea I've been here before," she said softly. "Do I have a bed?" She caught her mother's quick nod. "Good," she said. "Then I shall go and lie down. Call me when it's time for the visit to court. I believe the king is waiting for me."

CHAPTER FIVE

Being a member of staff and not an honoured resident, Rosie did not live in two large and beautifully decorated rooms. However, as daughter of the owner, her bedchamber was larger than many. Without help, she scrambled from her clothes, flung them to the stool in the corner, but missed, so that most ended on the floor. She then clambered beneath the nice linen sheet, which she had originally ironed herself, the two woolly blankets, and the eiderdown emblazoned with pictures of crows, which she had embroidered herself many years ago. Then Rosie snuggled up, head on pillow, shut her eyes and slept without movement for thirteen hours.

Meanwhile Dickon, Dipper Jaws the gardener, Bert Cackle and Harry Flash gathered outside and dug holes. Having rained, the ground was soft. The spades, however, were mostly cracked due to long disuse. Dipper, it seemed, did not do as much gardening as he was paid for. Yet, the digging continued, and soon a grave-sized hole sat mid-lawn. Between them, they collected the parts of the body still sufficiently connected, and dropped them in the grave.

They then slung all the mud back on top and patted down the end result. It was a bit of a mess, but they assumed it would tidy itself up in time. Lemony stuck a lilac twig at the head and waved a cheerful cheerio.

With dutiful reverence, Dickon managed the words he'd promised. "Ashes to ashes and dust to dust," he said, but had forgotten the rest.

"Have a nice sleep," Peg added.

"And don't take a wrong turning and end up in purgatory," Emmaline recommended. "You wouldn't like it. Make sure you read the proper sign posts."

"Oh, gracious no." Alice advised. "Don't go getting lost." And then she thought of something else. "And don't come back."

Believing his work done for the day, Dickon marched off, sorry only that he had not been able to say goodbye to the gorgeous girl in satin who evidently liked to lay down on doorsteps.

Life tick-tocked back almost to normal that night. The moon made a brief appearance but then went off behind the clouds in private, the stars glittered and stayed there, not having been given any choice, Cabbage the owl flew off to discover a few mice, the crows nestled down into their big bundled black beds, some with eggs, some with chicks and some comfy just for themselves. The bats flew from the holes under the roof and flapped into the night, and the occupants of The Rookery climbed into their own beds, ready to snore until morning.

When Rosie woke the following dawn, she had a slight headache and hurried downstairs for breakfast. Having wandered into the kitchen, she grabbed one of the empty buckets, said good morning to her mother, and asked if she should go off to the well.

Somewhat surprised when her mother turned in startled amazement, Rosie asked. "What's the matter? Have I grown a third eye?"

"What did you say first?" Alice demanded.

Now thoroughly perturbed, Rosie muttered, "I only said good morning, Mamma. What's wrong with that?"

Peg had been standing, her back to the kitchen, staring out at the garden through the window, contemplating Whistle's grave. Now she turned in a hurry. "What's your name?" she asked at once.

Now even more confused and definitely worried, Rosie answered, "Why, Rosie, of course. Have you gone mad?"

"I have always been mad," Peg replied with dignity. "But I was concerned that you might be going the same way."

"And who am I?" Alice asked, her voice trembling.

"Who? What? I don't understand," Rosie trembled. "You're my mother, and your name is Alice. What on earth is wrong with you all this morning?" And she put down the bucket, having remembered something. "And there's a crumpled old heap of rags on my bedroom floor. Where did that come from?"

Everyone stared at everyone else.

The pile of rags on Rosie's bedchamber floor did not contain the lush extravagance of clothes that Rosie had been wearing the day before. Rags were rags, and these were rags. Most appeared to be torn pieces of old mops, some ripped corners of shift or shirt. Unravelling threads of wool and a ribbon cut into many tiny pieces completed the heap.

"This," Peg announced, "has changed considerably in the night. Now what I'd like to know is whatever you can remember."

"So would I." Rosie shook her head. "I would never have gone collecting this sort of rubbish, so surely someone else had put it there while I was asleep. A bit worrying, I suppose, but nothing urgent."

Peg regarded her younger friend. "I do believe," she said, fumbling with her fingers, "Something is missing. You may feel normal, my dear, but a few events have fallen out of the basket. We shall discuss this later."

"Down at the Juggler and Goat?"

"Well, you certainly remember some things," Peg nodded. "But today I do believe we should stay in and not drink quite so much."

Rosie frowned. "I only had an ale and a small Burgundy. It was you who drank half the cellar dry."

"So, you do remember some of the evening." Peg smiled without shame. "But there's something a good deal more important to dredge up."

The sun had risen in pink pastels, and now a mild warmth was drying off the garden. Having finished breakfast, a rather dreary one of porridge without added milk, bread without butter or marmalade, and mugs of ale without any taste at all since Alice had been far too distracted to produce any decent cooking, nor decent magic either, Peg led Rosie out to the old wooden bench outside, overlooking the newly dug grave.

Peg then explained what, as yet unexplained, had happened yesterday. "I never believe what clocks try to tell me," Peg finished, "so I don't know how long you were away. But a long time, that's for sure. And when you came back, you were dafter than I am."

But Rosie did not at first remember a single moment, and they both sat in puzzled silence, watching the sun flourish and fly upwards, soon proclaiming midday.

"I suppose," said Rosie at last, "it might just have been your magic going wrong again?"

Peg was not amused. "I wasn't doing magic at that moment – not a single flick. And besides, my spells are never quite that ridiculous. Now look at Whistle," and she pointed to the muddy brown lumps in the grass. "He was undoubtedly killed by a complete stranger. I am perfectly sure the same complete stranger, with considerable magical power, swooped down to take you on a strange journey, then completely wiped it from your memory. Not only do we not have the faintest idea who he is, but why bash poor Whistle, and then take you on a fun trip?"

"Maybe he likes me. He didn't like Whistle."

"Then undoubtedly this freak is male," Peg decided. "But what has your pleasant evening got to do with Whistle's death?" Then, after a very brief pause, she added, "I shall have to use my own magic, dear, and do what one day in the future they'll call hypnotism."

Rosie was dubious. "And what does *hipnotodism* do? I refuse to stand on my head or bury myself with Whistle or anything else horrible."

"You just sit there quietly, like the sweet little child you are." Peg grinned at her. She stood, flapped both arms beyond the confines of her cape, stared up for a moment into the clouds and their golden linings, clicked her fingers on both hands and looked down on Rosie's questioning expression. The crows were squawking, and one, interested, swept down to sit on Peg's shoulder. She pushed it away and pointed one finger at Rosie.

Immediately, Rosie closed her eyes.

"Now what," Peg asked in a dulcet command, "happened to you yesterday evening between leaving the Juggler and Goat and arriving back to sleep in your bedchamber? Please explain. I wish to hear a nice long story." When complete silence followed, Peg added, "Please start from the beginning, and please speak aloud." One final thought occurred. "And what did you do with all those lovely ruby and pearl hair pins?"

Flopping a little sideways, Rosie spoke as though chanting a lesson from the bible. "I found myself walking through a forest. Nice green trees and a warm breeze. I stepped on bluebells. Down the slope, there was a stream. A frog looked at me and made a funny noise. Then it splashed back into the water. I walked on. A stag watched me, but no one else was around. So I took off my smock and walked into the stream. It was chilly but felt nice, so I sat down, and the ripples came over my shoulders. The stag came over, but I told it to go away. Then it told me I was pretty, and I said, thank you! The frog was on my knee. It said it was a prince in disguise, and promised to give me pretty new clothes.

"When I climbed out of the water, the stag blew all over me with his nice warm breath until I was dry, and the frog hopped over to a neat folded pile of clothes. I started to put them on, and they were very pretty and special. I thanked the frog and the stag most politely. '*Now you're a princess,*' the frog told me. '*Go and sit on your throne.'* So I did. The clothes were lovely, and as I got dressed, the frog leapt around whistling at me. I walked away into the forest until I saw the nice stone doorstep and recognised it as my throne. So I sat there and felt very comfy."

Looking up, Peg realised she had an audience. Standing behind the bench, and listening avidly, were Mandrake, Emmeline and Montague, with Harry peeping from behind. On the other side stood Alice and Lemony, whilst staring down from the windows above were every other member of The Rookery. There were a few crows poking their beaks down as well.

Peg clapped her hands, Rosie woke and sat up, and Alice said, "Make her remember. I want to know more."

"I remember everything now," Rosie said, smiling into the sunshine. "It was fun. I must have looked so nice with my hair all specially done and those pretty hairpins. But it got all messed up again in the night. And all the clothes have gone."

"And the pins?"

"Unfortunately, yes."

"But," frowned Mandrake, "you mentioned the frog whistling. I wonder if that means anything."

"But Whistle never whistled," Peg murmured.

Rosie shook her now unpinned hair. "And why would Whistle's ghost give me a nice afternoon out in a place that doesn't exist?"

It was Kate who found the one remaining hairpin that afternoon. Being the maid, a small drooping female parented by a witch and a wizard many centuries past, but who had unfortunately been born with virtually no magical skills whatsoever, she worked in The Rookery as maid and washer-upper, even though Rosie did most of it anyway. But Kate was making Rosie's bed, and there, under the pillow, was a bright shining ruby stuck on the end of a silver pin. Sharp, glittery and gorgeous. Kate paused, wondering whether she should steal it, but decided that a household of folk who could read your mind and turn you into a tadpole would not make stealing a safe business after all the mystery, murder and mayhem.

So she trotted off to where Rosie still sat in the garden with Peg and presented it to her. "Under your pillow, mistress."

Between them Peg and Rosie prodded this unexpected find, dug it into each other with various squeaks and other complaints, pointed it at Whistle's grave, imbedded it into the grass and finally clutched it while muttering spells. Nothing interesting eventuated from any of the practises, and Peg sighed. "Pretty, my dear, and all yours. Valuable, too, I should think. But it is just an ordinary jewel and offers no unusual insights."

"Unexpected, though," decided Rosie. "How many did I have yesterday? Ten? Fifteen? And only this one managed to survive. I feel it has to be special." She tucked the silver spike through the neck of her smock. "I'll wait and see if anything happens."

When Peg trotted into the kitchen for a hot dinner, Rosie ignored her appetite, knowing the dinner would be fairly disgusting anyway, and sat stroking the hat pin stuck into her smock beneath her chin. "I wonder if you could tell me something," she said aloud. "Tell me – if you have one, your name?"

It had only been one of many possibilities, and she had expected no reply. She was exceedingly startled when a gruff little voice said, "Oswald."

Jerking around, Rosie quickly saw that she sat alone, and no one else could have supplied that voice, except the ruby pin. So she tingled with excitement and murmured, "And number two, did you come from that forest and that stream where I went yesterday?"

"Of course," said the voice with an impatient rasp. "What else, for goodness sake. I couldn't have floated from your chimney, now, could I?"

Magic, Rosie acknowledged, was invariably impatient and fairly bad tempered. She asked, "So number three, why did you stay when all the other pins disappeared?"

"They weren't real," said Oswald. "But I'm real, and I came on loan. Loaned, remember! Not a gift."

"Oh." Somewhat disappointed, Rosie asked, "And so number four, borrowed from who?"

"Wait and see," muttered the little gruff voice under her chin. "Now, I'm not here for fun, you know. There's motive and mystery, and we have to get into it together. Yes, yes, I know, you're only a fifty, but your friend Peg is an eighty-seven."

"Eighty-five."

"Don't you start arguing with me," snapped the pin. "If I say she's an eighty-seven, then that's what she is. Me – I'm a ninety-nine. So let's get started."

"At what?" Rosie was even more confused than usual.

"Finding out who killed me – I mean, Whistle Hobb," said the ruby pin in a hurry.

Having to wait for Peg to return from the kitchen, Rosie went for a rare walk alone around the garden. Long pebbled paths ran between clipped hedges and a few bushes of meadow sweet, lilac and briar roses. Surrounding this were the varied trees, each holding its own collection of rookery bundles, with the nesting crows content within. Many of the birds were pleasant companions, but at present considered themselves far too busy to waste time chatting with wingless people. One crow, however, flew down to Rosie's shoulder and peered over to stare at the magical pin.

"Red," observed Tubbs, who was extremely black himself.

"Of course. It's a ruby," Rosie pointed out.

Tubbs risked a quick peck. "Interesting."

The pin was still thinking of something rude to say when Peg returned, trotting down the garden path with a wide smile.

"Your news first," Rosie said, her own smile equally as wide as Peg's. "Then I'll tell you mine."

"My news?" Peg looked at Rosie and the crow on her shoulder, and her smile turned to a frown. "None, I'm afraid. Just that dinner was nicer than usual. We had pasties and buttery leeks. Quite pleasant."

"Sit down then," Rosie told her, "and I'll be able to relate all mine." She flicked at Tubbs, who flew off. Then Rosie began. "My dear Peg, let me start with number one."

CHAPTER SIX

Peg was gapping, and her bright black eyes were luminous. "My dear girl," she said with a vigorous nod, "You will soon double your fifty. This is most interesting and quite amazing. I've tottered this somewhat boring country for some years, and no hat pin has ever spoken to me before."

"And all for me!" Rosie said, breathy with excitement. "Flitting off yesterday, and the ruby hat pin this morning. And I'm just a below average fifty. I always felt a little ashamed of myself, plodding around with a mop and bucket. People looked at me and asked when supper would be ready, or why hadn't I washed up the spilled wine in the meeting hall or I should go and clean the moss from the front doorstep because it was slippy."

"You did that yesterday," Peg said, and regretted it. "No, no, dear. It was all your idea to find whoever killed Whistle – such a sensible kindness. And so the reward is yours. And besides," Peg added, "whoever told you about just being a fifty?"

"My mother." Rosie had been ten, the normal age for the test and the following investiture. With a fifty mother and a lowly father who could claim only twenty, Rosie had not expected much, but had hoped and hoped and hoped, and had even asked the great Whistle to help her increase her score.

'Not something I can do with a little girl,' he had told her. 'Lessons afterwards, perhaps, if your mother doesn't keep you permanently in the kitchen grating the carrots. But there are often surprises. You may have a higher score than you expect.'

Rosie had never been asked to grate a carrot, but she had certainly been partially glued to the kitchen. As an excited little ten-year-old girl, she had hoped and hoped. But her score had been a lowly fifty, as expected.

"How could you have expected more than me, stupid girl?" spat her mother. So no investiture was to follow.

With the sunshine melting away behind the clouds, Peg took Rosie's elbow, and followed the pebble path back to The Rookery. The birds were busy, swooping and diving while their babies hollered for food, more food and more food. By now most of the well snuggled eggs had hatched, and so each nest held four or five babies, each convinced it was about to starve to death. Mothers, fathers and older siblings answered the call, and all local insects did a quick run. Some of the witches chucked out their unwanted crusts, the occasional edge of burned pastry and a few fishy skins for the crows to find, and Harry Flash studied a whole new idea and invented what appeared to be uncooked frogs' legs, even though they had never been worn by a single frog. They had popped out of Harry's upside-down hat.

Rosie and Peg had just arrived at the back door into the kitchen, when a scruffy little fledgling plopped at their feet, having presumably fallen from its nest.

Looking up, dismayed, Rosie waved. "Mistress crow," she called, "one of the clutch has left home a little early. It certainly can't fly yet. Who does it belong to?"

The fledgling might not yet be capable of flying, but it was quite skilled at hopping. It was now pecking at Rosie's toes. A faint but distracted voice tumbled from above. "I have all mine, dear. Four little brats and one egg still to go."

Another cawed loudly. "I don't want any more. I have six. Quite enough."

The third mother crow flapped, zoomed down and regarded the homeless baby. "No, not mine," she said. "My poor husband Wolfy has a bad wing after trying to catch one of those big mean spiders, and I have to go hunting while he sits on the nest. It's exhausting. But there's just one hatchling left to pop out."

Scooping up the fledgling from the ground, Peg gazed at the irate piece of uncombed fluff in her hand. "You," she told it, "seem you have dropped out of nowhere. Perhaps I had better adopt you and feed you myself."

The fledgling hopped up and down, flapped the few scraggy bits of feather it owned and cawed with approval. Rosie nodded vigorously. "I was about to say the same thing," she said. "Isn't it sweet." And with sudden determination the baby hopped from Peg's hand and onto Rosie's shoulder. It then proceeded to peck her ear lobe. She refused to admit that this hurt and turned to Peg. "Do you mind?" she asked. "I'd love to keep him."

Peg didn't mind. "He's sweet. But I have enough to do."

Half in and out of the kitchen already, they hurried indoors. Hoping not to be stopped and scalded by her mother, Rosie stuffed the little squirming lump in her apron pocket and ran up the stairs to her own room. Peg, moaning at the stairs, hobbled behind.

"There's a reason for this," Peg blurted, sinking down on the bed. "Just as we said a few moments ago. You – my dear – are getting all the attention. Is it possible that you're being coached?"

"Someone's trying to make me cleverer than I really am?" Rosie patted the squirming lump in her white linen apron as Peg smiled at the same little lump. It did not exactly look ready to teach anything to anyone.

"Have you seen your father lately?" Peg asked abruptly.

It was a matter of frequent shame. "No." Rosie shook her head.

"He likes to be left alone, you see. Lives a very solitary life, dear Papa."

"I have a sudden desire to visit him," said Peg. "Bring Whatsit with you, and we'll find a few beetles for him. But it's your father I need to talk with. Alfred Scaramouch, isn't it? Good." She raised both hands, fingers ready to click. "Where does this solitary gentleman live, then?"

"I don't want to call him Whatsit."

"What?" Peg hiccupped.

"My little baby crow," said Rosie,

Peg sat back down on the side of the bed. "I have an idea," she said. "Beatles first, I suppose."

"My father doesn't eat beetles."

Each gazed at the other in confusion. Finally Peg said, "My dear girl, you, me and the baby crow will now visit your father. I think he's up to something."

"My lovely sweet father," Rosie insisted, "would never do anything as disgusting as killing Whistle Hobb. Besides, he'd never manage it."

"I would never suspect such a thing. Take me to your father. Now," sighed Peg, "not another word. Let's fly immediately."

"I've changed my mind about calling my baby Sam," Rosie murmured to herself. "I think Splodge is better. More suited. He lives in a tree house."

Peg glared. "So your father has changed his name to Splodge and Sam will live in a treehouse?"

"Try the other way around," said Rosie. "Look, up there, in the great big ash tree." She pointed towards the tiny window. "Daddykins built his tree house out there ages ago. I was tiny when father set to and built his house. He's lived there ever since."

"Now this," grinned Peg, "is going to be interesting. I've lived here since before the Battle of Agincourt, so why did I never know anything about your father?"

"He's not very sociable," Rosie apologised.

"But he'll let us in?"

Rosie hoped so. "If I remind him that I'm his daughter."

"Very well," Peg said. "It's even higher than most of the crows' nests, so we might as well leave directly through the window. Can you open it? I'm a little tired of my forehead decorated in purple bruises."

Rosie obligingly reached outwards, pushing the tiny window wide open on both sides. She stuck her head out, although there was barely enough space, and certainly not enough for her shoulders. "Are you sure?"

"Quite sure," Peg said. "Now take my hand."

Without time for breath or blink, Rosie discovered herself sitting on the wide branch of a tree, its new fresh springtime greenery burgeoning all around and smelling of rebirth. Rosie had never sat so enclosed by growth as previous visits to her father had involved her calling him down. The floor of the house sat next to their shoulders, strongly slatted and balancing on four ash branches. With a hop as good as Splodge's, Peg landed on the small porched entrance and knocked on the door.

The knocker was a carved wooden owl, and the porch was held by two carved pillars, a dozen different birds seeming to climb the rigid height. Peg was impressed, lifted the somewhat useless letter box flap and called, "Master Scaramouch, I don't wish to inconvenience you, but we've come for a most important visit. I'm Peg Tipple, and here waiting beside me is your dear daughter Rosie."

To Rosie's surprise and relief, the door opened immediately.

CHAPTER SEVEN

The house looked marvellous, but Alfred Scaramouch did not. His eyes were bloodshot, and he seemed far more exhausted than any wizard had any right to appear.

"Well, well, well." He rubbed his hands together and smiled through all the wrinkles. "My little girl and her little friend." His beard, thick, very white, and reaching a little past his waist, was quivering with evident delight. "You are most welcome indeed. Although," and his voice partially disappeared into his beard, "I am not at my best. Not that I have any idea what my best might be, but this isn't it. The nesting season, you see."

Ushering his guests into the one huge room beyond the porch, the old wizard pointed to several slightly broken and tooth marked chairs, inviting them to sit. Then, with a huge exhale, he also sat, crossing his arms and stretching his legs below his long blue robe.

The slight problem with the interesting room was the generous coating of feathers floating down, claw clippings, bits of scraggy nesting materials, bird seed and spiders' webs. Looking around, it occurred to Rosie that an equally unexpected quagmire of odds and flickers also adorned her father's beard. She brushed a couple of feathers and a small white mouse from her chair, and addressed her father. "Hello, Papa. I'm so pleased to see you again. It's been – ages. I can't remember how long. But I'm not much good at flying upwards, you see. And I don't think I'd be much good at climbing either. "

"I brought her," said Peg with brief practicality.

Splodge, still tucked into Rosie's apron, managed a plaintive squawk. "Nesting time, of course," continued Alfred, picking a small piece of fluff down from an eyelash, "is my busiest. I help feeding when I can. I mean, you can't expect all these poor little birds to do it on their own. And then the babies. They need an occasional cuddle too, you know."

Splodge proved the point, spoking his knobbly little head and wide eyes up into the light and hopped to Alfred's lap, as if this had been his intention all along.

"Umm," said Rosie. "We found him."

"I thought I'd lost him," said Alfred. "Thank you for bringing him back."

"I see you are keeping up the magical practise," approved Peg.

But Alfred shook his head, which tangled his beard with his hair. "Oh, dear me, no," he smiled. "I still do a little, of course. I used a good deal back when I built this house. But not since. I can't even fly, you see, but I manage some things I find necessary. I have an attic bedchamber which I share with the bats," he pointed to the ceiling, "and just concern myself with the delightful creatures I find around here. Baby crows that get lost. Some of those yellow long-legged spiders are good company naturally, and I have plenty of excellent conversations with the owls. Cabbage is a real charmer, you know. But," and he leaned back in his chair with a joyous smile, "I'm waiting for the swallows to arrive."

With no idea what to say in answer to this, Rosie kept quite silent, but Peg was eager, squinty-eyed, and ready to talk. "Yes, yes," she said. "All very nice for those of us who have nothing better to do. But, for instance, did you know that very recently poor Whistle Hobb was slaughtered? Oh yes, bashed to tiddly bits."

Alfred raised one very careful eyebrow. "Do I know him?"

"Of course you do," Peg told him rather crossly. "He was the most powerful wizard in the whole Rookery. And," she added, "I'm the second."

"I imagine I'm at the bottom of the steps in the wood chippings and the hen droppings," smiled Alfred.

Peg was about to be polite, but Rosie cut in. "I expect you're stronger now, Papa. Talking to the birds and so forth."

"We all talk to the crows," he pointed out. "They're real chatter-boxes. And the owls of course. You can't get a word in when Cabbage is on a rant."

"I have never spoken to a yellow spider," said Rosie, who wasn't sure if she'd actually ever seen one.

"But on the other hand," Peg interrupted, raising the other hand, "if you'd felt lately that your magic is – fading. Just a little, perhaps. One point or two on the slide. Twenty down to sixteen, let's suppose, just as an example."

"Humph. Possible," said the magician without evident interest. "I'm quite happy as I am, you know. A visit from my darling daughter is certainly a pleasant little moment to anticipate. Old friends – new friends – and all the beauty of the forest. That's all I need. Oh, just enough magic for a vegetarian pottage every now and again of course."

"Just a small point," Peg leaned forwards, nose twitching, "but you never answered the question about Whistle Hobb. Did you know he was dead? Not just dead, but actually killed?"

The beard wobbled as Alfred shook his head. "I can't even remember the man," he said. "But sorry to hear about it. Killing just isn't nice. I tell the crows not to kill the poor little rats. People call them vermin, but they're just sweet little animals like everything else."

"You've been most helpful," said Peg at once, standing up. "Thank you, Master Alfred. I shall visit again one day."

"Not too often," added Alfred in alarm.

Staring at Peg, Rosie sat where she was. "We've only just arrived." She turned back to her father. "Look at all those pretty tapestries. Look at the dear little steps, all made of crows' nests, leading up to the attic bedroom. And the best must be looking out of that great big window at the tree tops. That's just glorious. I'd love to live here myself."

"Oh, dear me, no," said her father in a hurry. "I'm sure you wouldn't like it, dear. There's no kitchen, you know."

Trying to remember, Rosie realised she actually couldn't remember much at all. "How long have you lived here?" she asked. "Always? Forever? Or just a couple of years? I thought I could remember you building here when I was a baby, but how can I remember being just a few months old?"

"Neither forever – a difficult concept since I haven't been alive forever. But a lot more than a few years." Alfred smiled.

"Don't worry, Daddykins," Rosie assured him, and stood beside Peg. "I suppose we should be leaving, and you can go back to the peace you love. Say hello to Cabbage for me." And she patted Splodge, who turned his back. Rosie decided she wouldn't miss him after all.

He saw them out, his beard now parting slightly as a bright yellow spider peeped out, saw Peg and darted back amongst the thick white hair. "Be careful, and do enjoy whatever it is you usually enjoy," Alfred called after them. "Come again in a year or so. And now I shall get my trumpet ready to frighten away any eagles that think of taking a chick for dinner."

This time Peg flew herself and Rosie down to the back garden, and Peg stared over at Whistle Hobb's grave. "I wonder," she said.

"You wonder what?"

"I had an idea, but your father didn't confirm it." Yet Peg pulled a face and screwed up her long, hooked nose. "Well, not willingly. But in a way, he did. Why in the name of all that's wiccan, did he pretend he never knew Whistle? Everybody did. I wish to speak to your mother. I need a few more facts."

"I don't see how any of this helps us find out who killed poor Whistle," Rosie objected.

"We take the ladder one titchy step at a time," Peg told her, the smug smile of knowing more than she was yet inclined to explain was sitting wide. "Come along. We've done Daddykins. Now let's chat with Mummykins."

"I've never called her that," Rosie muttered. "She's not the type."

Alice Scaramouch sat, one eye shut, on a kitchen stool with her back resting against the wall where various pots and pans were hanging higher up. Her one eye shut meant she was sleeping, and her one eye open indicated that she still knew what was going on around her.

"Ah," Peg said, very loudly as she marched into the kitchen from the garden. "What a pleasant surprise. Just who I wanted to talk to."

Opening the other eye, Alice stared, disgruntled. "Why?"

"Oh, ancient history and a few other things," she said. "And I have a few questions regarding your dear daughter. I just had the pleasure of visiting your husband. Have you seen Alfred lately?"

"Not for a few years," sniffed Alice. "Six or seven maybe. But the crows would tell me if he'd dropped dead or caught malaria."

"And would it seem dreadfully odd," Peg asked sweetly, "if I was to ask you all about Rosie's birth. Your only child. Such a drama, I'm sure. You must remember."

"Of course I remember," Alice snapped. "Doesn't mean I want to talk about it. The greatest pain a woman ever has, you know. Well, of course, you wouldn't know. There's few witches have children these days. There's few who even get married, let alone do the mother thing. So buzz off and talk to the crows about their eggs, and what a fuss and bother it is feeding the silly little things every year."

"I presume," Peg sat opposite as if starting an interrogation, "you feel quite proud of yourself being one of our few actual mothers?"

"Why not?" demanded Alice with a curdled smile. "Now if

you're writing a history book or something, get on with the questions. I haven't got all day."

"Actually, you have several days," Peg replied. "But I only want to know about Rosie's ten years test. She came out as a fifty, as we all know now. But who did the test? Was it the official tester? And was it a straight fifty? No little scaramouch tails on the end?"

"Oh, this is so boring," frowned Alice. "Let me try and remember. Yes, Rosie was ten. Her tenth birthday, as is proper. It was all very conventional, you know. And, yes, it was a straight fifty."

"Who did the test?" Peg insisted.

"Oh, I don't remember that. It might have been Whistle himself," Alice said, clearing her throat as though uncomfortable in some way. "But I'm afraid I lost the papers years back."

"And you haven't summoned their return?"

"Not important enough," Alice was getting impatient. "If you think Rosie is not a fifty any longer, then test her yourself. It couldn't be official, naturally. But for you to satisfy this irritating curiosity."

"I do so like to irritate," said Peg. "I might just do that. I would have supposed it was that Edna person. Edna Edith Elsie Ethel or something like that. She did all the tests before she flew off to some cave in Scotland."

"Never heard of her," grumbled Alice.

"Really?" Peg's grin turned into a cackle. "Sounds like your dear husband whose name you've probably forgotten, who said he'd never met Whistle. In the meantime, exactly when is Rosie's birthday? Now don't tell me you've lost that as well?"

The deep crimson flush rising from jaw to eyes was a reasonable indication of how the irritation was affecting Alice. "Ridiculous," she mumbled. "Of course I remember. I was there, wasn't I?"

"And?"

Rosie, standing quietly behind Peg, was tempted to interrupt since she knew her birthdate perfectly well, but she snapped her mouth shut again and lowered her eyes to her lap.

Alice meanwhile said loudly, "Absurd, Mistress Peg. That's enough. Why didn't you ask Alfred if you were over there a minute ago? I'll answer this and no more. Rosie was born on the ninth of June. Umm, yes, twenty-three years ago. Now, satisfied? Good, I have work to do now. Goodbye."

And she scuttled off, disappearing into the garden with an empty basket she had quickly grabbed on the way out.

Peg looked at Rosie, and Rosie's mouth had fallen open again. Peg grinned. "Well, my dear," she said. "I hope you found that most interesting?"

Rosie gulped. "So my mother has a bad memory. That's not important," Rosie muttered. "You keep forgetting things and get them muddled as well."

"But I hope I am right in saying your birthdate was the eighteenth of June when you'll turn twenty-five? And now you're twenty-four?"

Rosie nodded. "But who cares? I don't care about my mother. Never have. She's looked after me for years, and I'm grateful, but she's no darling. Anyway, the important thing is Whistle's death, and none of this about me has any relevance at all." Rosie felt upset and said so. "You've just made me feel even more rotten about my stupid mother, which doesn't matter in the slightest. I care about Whistle. So let's get on with it."

"You don't want the test?" Peg asked with a sniff. "I have no official permission to do the test, but I'm perfectly capable, you know."

"Like the occasional visit to the Gobi Desert?"

"Oh, pooh," Peg's nose twitched several times. "Anyway, it wouldn't prove anything. So, come with me, my dear."

"Where?"

A stubborn desire had left Rosie with a stubborn desire expression. "Nothing more about me," she said through her teeth.

"No more me, me, me or my mother or even my father. Only and strictly just Whistle."

Peg sighed. "Come on then, my dear. Whistle's bedchamber it is." And she clicked the fingers of her right hand, flying Rosie and herself from the back doorstep up to the top floor where the grandeur of Whistle's two rooms still remained vacant.

Both rooms had been cleaned and tidied. A strong cider and wet parsnip smell pervaded. Kate, the maid, had clearly used her homemade disinfectant. The bedchamber seemed surprisingly banal. Without any hint of the previous occupant, the bed was made, the table top was empty, the shelves were neat and the Turkey rug on the floor lay flat.

They wandered through to the second chamber and gazed at the nothingness. A chair and two stools stood around an empty hearth, another rug beneath and another empty table off to the side.

"Bother," said Rosie.

Peg said a lot more, but kept the words under her breath. Finally, she shrugged, nodded for Rosie to take her hand and follow, and flew down the stairs to the ground floor at the back, just beyond the courtyards where the abandoned stables had been taken over by the staff, both Kate and Dipper now lodging there.

Knocking on Kate's door first, Peg pushed the way open and marched inside. "Right," she said. "What have you done with all Whistle's papers and books and scrolls?"

Once again outside amongst the crows and other birds, Rosie smiled. She could understand very well why her father had taken to the trees. The rustle and song were far more beautiful than the shouting and the kitchen bell within the building. But, as her father had shown, Kate was not overjoyed at being so abruptly visited. She wiped her hands on her apron, sniffed onto her sleeve, and made a sort of haphazard curtsey. "I weren't skiving orff," she said. "'Tis my time fer meself."

"Just a friendly visit," Peg assured her. "Now, what have you done with all Whistle Hobb's papers? Quick, and we'll leave you in peace."

"I ain't stole nuffing."

"Prove it, and hand them over," said Peg.

Kate scowled. "Torn up and burned," she said. "Mistress Alice done ordered it, and she done lit the fire fer me an' all. So I ain't got nuffing."

Peg stepped backwards with an expression of fury mixed with disappointment. "My own stupid fault," she muttered to herself. "I had those things in my hands. All of them. And I let them go. Botheration and diddley-poo with horns on." She turned back to Kate. "When you cleaned up," she said with an encouraging smile which seemed distinctly false, "did you see anything odd you can tell me about? And better still, have you kept anything?" She paused, then added, "I shall pay to get it back, whatever it is."

"I done gived it all to Mistress Alice," Kate said. "Now I ain't got nuffing. But yous can pay me anyways."

"Tell me *what* you remember?" Peg pleaded, attempting a softer approach. "It's most important. Just try."

She sighed, still frowning at Peg. Rosie was sitting in the corner, gazing out of the window at the crows. She wished she could join her father and go and feed them.

"Jumble and rumble," muttered Kate. "There were papers o' so many kinds it were real tedious, and they all done shouted at me. I screwed 'em up. That shut the little moaners up. Then there were scales what I dropped and broke, and Master Hobb's cape what wouldn't sit still. Some stuff were silver, and I knows as how that were proper valuable, so I gived it all to Mistress Alice."

"Really?" Peg smiled faintly.

"There were little tufty things and scoopy stuff. I reckon there was some o' the gent's brains, but I just wiped that up an' all."

"Oh, very well," Peg said. "Just one thing more. Give me the two silver items you stole, and I shall give you two honest sovereigns."

Kate blinked. "Not made up coin what's gonna fade out tomorrow?"

"No. The real stuff. And not a single word to Alice. Just a secret between us."

Kate bustled off and returned with a clutch of silver, which she stuffed into Rosie's apron pocket with a snicker. "Right. Where's me dosh?"

Peg handed over the two golden sovereigns, and leaving Kate to gloat over her coins, Peg and Rosie left the stables and flew back up to Peg's bedchamber.

CHAPTER EIGHT

P eg stretched out both hands and stared at the silver items she held, one in each. One small pile of glitter appeared to be a misshapen silver toadstool. Peg's right hand clutched something far larger. This was a spoon, big enough to feed an overgrown ox. She laid both objects beside her on the bed and stared, then rubbed her index finger carefully over each one. She whispered at both, held one and blew on the other, swapped over, and eventually pointed at one after the other and demanded, "Explain yourselves."

The spoon was reflecting Peg's pursed mouth. It had a deep voice. "You may have noticed," it said, "that I'm a spoon."

The toadstool sniggered. "He's fibbing," it said. "He's a clock. Tells the time, the date and the past. Sometimes, when he's in the right mood, he can tell the future."

Leaning forward with sudden delight, Rosie began to take an interest. "Brilliant," she said, ignoring Peg. "So who killed poor Whistle?"

"Not me," said the spoon at once. "And anyway, you'll have to wait for permission. In the meantime, you've got a visitor. Come back later."

The toadstool was sniggering again. "He's an arrogant spoon," it advised. "Needs a spoonful of wine, I expect."

When there was a knock on the main door downstairs. Peg cursed again. "Who is it?"

"The sheriff's assistant," said the spoon with a voice of vague boredom. "It's you lot he wants. I may see you later, unless I've gone back to sleep."

"Upstairs, downstairs, up and down, up and down," Peg complained. "Come on, my girl. Your admirer won't take long, I hope, and we can come back here."

"My admirer?" Rosie was not amused.

"Not only just a pathetic fifty," Peg shrugged, "but blind and deaf as well. Come on, dear. We'll fly."

Rosie was a little surprised at such unaccustomed insults, but with hands clasped tight to Peg's, she followed her down to the front door and watched as Alice opened it to Dickon, the same sheriff's assistant who had come two days previously. They showed him into the meeting hall where he sat and surveyed his audience.

With a quick sideways smile at Rosie, he turned back to Alice, saying, "Well, mistress, I must investigate this most unpleasant murder. So I need to interview every one of your residents."

Alice, Peg and Rosie all pulled a variety of faces, but there seemed little escape. "I shall send them in one at a time," Alice sighed. "But I warn you, Master Wald, my resident folk here are a somewhat eccentric bunch. Please don't judge them too harshly."

"And perhaps," he smiled sweetly again, "I could start with Mistress Rosie Scaramouch?"

Rosie sat. "I've been trying to work it out myself," she said at once. "And I've got nowhere. But I'm not giving up."

"And what were you doing that night?" the young man asked.

"Nothing." Rosie managed a half smile. "I mean, I was in bed. I always am at night. There's not much else to do."

"And have you discovered nothing from your own investigations, mistress?"

"Not a twinge."

"And who actually discovered the body?"

"Well," Rosie remembered, "actually, I think it was me. Except no, it must have been Kate before me." She bit her lip. "Not me. Kate. She's the maid. Or maybe my mother."

"I don't wish to be rude," Dickon said with an apologetic frown, "but this sounds a little like prevarication, Mistress Rosie."

"I don't care what it sounds like," Rosie objected. "My mother told me Whistle was dead. He'd died in the night. She told me to go and clean up so we could rent the rooms out again. So I did. There was an awful mess, and Whistle was smashed up really badly. I liked Whistle, but I never knew him very well. Then I ran back downstairs, and my mother got the maid to clean up instead."

"So how did your mother know in the beginning?"

Rosie thought about it. "She has quite good – instincts," she smiled, determined to go and ask her mother the same question.

After leaving the interview, Rosie ran outside again, avoiding both Alice and Peg for a few moments. She needed to think and squatted down beside Whistle's grave. "I do wish," she mumbled, "you could come and tell me what happened."

"Well," muttered a small gravelly voice from beneath her chin, "what do you think I'm here for? Just to decorate your collar? Very pretty, I'm sure, but I have better things to do than just tickle your chin."

Startled, Rosie nearly fell over. But she knew exactly who had spoken, and it wasn't Whistle. "You're a very nice hat-pin," she told it, one finger rubbing gently over the ruby. "But you weren't here when Whistle was murdered. If you can tell me anything magically, then I'd be most grateful. But how could I be sure whether to believe you?"

"Please yourself," said the hat-pin. "I'm quite content to go back to sleep. Admittedly the view just under your chin gets a little monotonous, but I won't complain."

"You just did," Rosie pointed out.

There was no answer, and she sat back, cross-legged, on the damp grass. It was true, of course, that her mother had been the first to speak of Whistle's death, but presumably someone had told her, since she was not one to make early morning visits, and she certainly never went to clean or tidy anyone else's bed. Yet Kate, when finally ordered to do the whole job, had not known what a terrible task she had been given. And Rosie couldn't remember anyone else who had known of the death before she did – just her own mother. And her mother was already in with Dickon Wald when she went to find her.

She bumped into Peg and accepted the inevitable. "So who actually discovered Whistle's body?" she demanded.

"Come with me," Peg said, grabbing her arm. "This time we have to get well away from the influences of the house. No Rookery. No Kettle Lane."

"The tavern?" Rosie quite liked the idea.

"Not even that." And Peg smiled. "Now, my dear. Close your eyes and breathe deep. We have to fly high, since we can't risk any of these boring mortals seeing us, especially Dickon the idiot."

Dutifully Rosie closed her eyes and smelled cold air and salt. She hoped it was dinner. But when she opened her eyes, she realised it was nothing of the sort.

The ocean swept before them. The soft blue waves echoed the sky and swirled gently into white froth as they climbed down to the beach. The tide was out, the day was calm, and the wind was a tiny breeze from the east. Beneath their feet, the sand was warm, and sailing through the tiny wisps of cloud above, the gulls wailed as they swooped. The brine smelled salty, of great journeys, of storms far off in the greater waves, and of strange shores.

Rosie clasped her hands together in delight. Visiting the English beaches was not an activity she had ever indulged. The ocean was for fishing, for the stark fear of adventure that ended in drowning, submerged beneath the unforgiving waters. Therefore, no one called the beach entertainment. Yet Rosie stood there now under the sun, and thought she had discovered another kind of magic.

"Exactly," said Peg, as though Rosie had spoken aloud. "And now I can start my own investigation. Are you comfortable? Good. Then I'll begin."

Keeping her eyes on the seemingly never-ending beauty before her, Rosie nodded. But when Peg began, Rosie interrupted. "Oh, not all about me again," she complained. "I thought we were going to investigate Whistle."

"We'll get to that," Peg insisted. "Now answer my question, dear. What do you remember of your magical test? I presume it was your tenth birthday?"

Lying back suddenly, Rosie clasped her hands behind her head, felt the soft nest of the sand beneath her and stared up at the sky and its family of swooping gulls. "I remember it in bits," she said patiently. "It was only fourteen years ago, but I must admit some of it is extremely wobbly. Bits up and holes down. To start with, I know it was my real birthday, and that's the first of July. Goodness knows why my stupid mother forgot my proper date and somehow dreamed up the ninth of June."

"A hint of problems to come," Peg murmured and continued, "So, my dear. Who was it exactly who monitored your test?"

"My mother was there." Rosie had closed her eyes. "I remember her standing at the back, looking cross. I expect she hoped I'd get a better result, but I didn't. I remember Whistle being there too, Not sure why. He stood beside my mother with a neat little smile. But the main person, very tall with one of those funny hats, was a stranger. I didn't know him at all, and I've never seen him since."

"That's the way it should be," Peg nodded. "Has to be someone over ninety him or herself, without knowledge or prejudice of the child being tested. Your mother should have remembered who it was, but it seems she has a remarkably poor memory."

"Since she's even forgotten my birthday."

"So carry on."

"I remember being flown to some sort of hall where the magician lived, I think, and being given a special cup of cold water, which was rather nice. Then I was told to sit still on a very high stool and – well – the rest is awfully hazy. But there was a strange woman, and then I remember getting home afterwards being absolutely exhausted and having to go to bed."

"A strange woman?" Peg mused. "Maybe Edna after all."

There was a brief interruption, a loud plop and then a screech. Rosie sat up and opened her eyes. Peg was running around in a circle with her cloak swirling in the opposite direction its own panic, both Peg's hands rummaging in her hair, before trotting down to the rippled edge of the water and scooping up handfuls to once again wipe into the straight white streaks on her head.

She eventually returned looking extremely bedraggled. Water dripped from the front of her head onto her nose, rolling on both sides of her nose down to her chin. The top of her head was soaked, but also seemed decorated by small plops of a sticky white substance. Her voluminous black cloak was clearly annoyed and continued to twitch and swish.

"What on earth?" asked Rosie.

"Piffle-down gliffle," mumbled Peg. "Wretched birds. Now, let's get on."

"There's nothing to get on with,' Rosie said at once. "That's all I remember."

"Impossible." Peg sat on the sand, salt water still dripping from her hair now landing in her lap. "Firstly, hold up both hands, palms outwards, and try to spread your fingers, making them as separate from each other as possible. Starting with the little finger on your right hand, mentally number them one to ten."

"One, two, I like numbers," Rosie said, dutifully obeying. "Seven, eight. Alright. Done."

"So point with number six. Quick," Peg told her. "Now eight. Now three. Well done."

"Does that make me magic?" Rosie asked. "Surely not. But I like numbers, and I do head-lists every morning. Number one, I have to fetch a bucket of water from the well. Number two, I have to make my bed and Mamma's. Number three—"

"I don't think we need any more," said Peg, waving her own fingers in the placid air. "It's not the numbers that matter. But never mind. Now, second question. You say you can't fly alone. Twaddle. Someone has put silly ideas in your head. Even a fifty can fly a little. So stand up. Good. Now jump up and down."

Feeling rather silly, Rosie did as she was told and jumped. "I feel ridiculous."

"You look it too," said Peg, "so carry on, but close your eyes and say after me, *'One cloud.' 'Second cloud.'*" Peg sniggered faintly, but then clapped her hands. "Well done, now open your eyes."

Having obeyed all instructions, Rosie opened her eyes, but was both amazed and extremely frightened when she discovered herself floating inside a damp white cloud, with a gull's feather stuck behind one ear and another in her shoe buckle. She tumbled down to earth immediately and landed with an unpleasant jolt. Standing quickly, she rubbed her backside.

"You could have warned me."

"Warned you that you have more powers than you think? And more than your mother told you?" Peg was now grinning. "But I have all I need to know, my girl. Excellent. So now we can go home. How about a short flight?"

CHAPTER NINE

"None of your business, my girl," Alice informed her daughter. "Now go and get on with your work. Have you made my bed yet?"

"Hours ago."

"Filled all three buckets?"

"Yes, of course. I do that every morning. But, Mamma, I only asked you what the human sheriff said." Rosie regarded her mother with fixed antagonism. "And while I'm asking one thing, I could ask another. How did you get my birthday wrong? Surely you remember the right day. You were there, after all."

"Stupid child." Alice had begun to produce a cauldron full of lamb and swede pottage, and a separate dish of lemon tart. Neither looked particularly appetising, although Alice worked hard enough, clicking her fingers and muttering into the little red sparks that appeared in the food. But the lemon tart, although looking quite smart, smelled of cow droppings and the pottage looked like unravelling wool.

Watching these procedures, Rosie asked, "Who did my coming of age test, Mother, when I was ten? And was it just a straight fifty?"

Whirling from pot to daughter, Alice glared. "Some old wizard did the test," she snapped. "I can't remember her name, Eleven Es or something, but she was very thorough and said it was a straight fifty without any extras. At least you weren't as low as your father. Then we just flew home."

The cauldron was bubbling and hubbling, but nothing smelled very nice. The fire beneath the trivet was energetic with huge golden flames, but it gave off very little heat. As a fifty as well, Alice did not produce miracles.

"And you forgot my birthday after all this time."

Alice turned back to stirring the pot. "Yes, yes, first of July, I do remember, silly girl. But, umm, it was the next year on the ninth of June when your father moved into his tree house. So both dates stay in my memory."

Accepting this, Rosie left the kitchen in a hurry, escaping the smell of a dinner she didn't think she was going to enjoy.

It was outside the meeting hall, door now fully open, that Dickon Wald bumped into Rosie. As he had only just emerged from the inner shadows, it seemed suspiciously as though he had been waiting for her, and the bumping accident was no accident at all. However, finding herself falling backwards, Rosie accepted the two solid arms which rescued her from the fall and supported her upright once again.

"Dear, dear," said Dickon. "My fault. I am dreadfully sorry." She smiled, and he leaned a little closer. "Can I make it up to you, Mistress Rosie? I should love to invite you out for a drink or a meal."

Remembering the smells wafting from the kitchen, Rosie said, "Well, perhaps a meal. I'd be grateful."

His narrow face stretched into a wide smile. "We could go to the Ordinary on the Green," Dickon said, opening the door for her as she stretched up and grabbed her cloak from the peg. "They do excellent pork pies."

"Or," said Rosie, wondering just how much of an idiot she was being, "we could go to the Juggler and Goat, I've heard they offer excellent food."

So they set off for the Juggler and Goat. Unfortunately, there was no way they could fly. However, it was a fine day, and the sun had not yet hidden for the night. Late spring meant long evenings, so it was already supper time. The tavern sounded a little noisy as they came closer, striding down Kettle Lane into the heart of Little Piddleton.

On his best behaviour, Dickon opened the tavern door for Rosie to hurry inside, and immediately the noise boomed out even louder, and the wave of heat was overpowering. But the couple sat at a tiny table in one corner, and Dickon waved a hand, managing to order two full suppers.

In order to fill in the wait without sitting there smiling inanely at each other, Rosie said, "I don't suppose you've managed to work out who our murderer is yet?

"Not something I should discuss with you, I'm afraid," said Dickon, sounding important.

"Well," Rosie said, smile in place, "just tell me which of our residents was most interesting to interview."

Evidently this invitation appealed. "One of your gentlemen borders," he confided, "is most impressive. Dandy Duckett, a most aged man but highly intelligent. Quite grand. I assume he comes from an excellent family who perhaps lost power during one of the past battles. I considered him quite a rare personality."

"A seventy-nine," Rosie remembered.

"Is that his age?" Dicken asked. "I knew he must be quite old, but that's a great age."

She hadn't been talking of his age, but she wasn't going to admit that now, especially since Dandy was probably two hundred and fifty years of age, or thereabouts. "He's – quite a nice old man," said Rosie. She'd never liked him.

"But Master Mandrake Karp, now he was a very different pond of fish. I found him highly suspicious."

"Ah," said Rosie, more interested and more in accord. "He's very arrogant. I don't like him either. But why did you find him suspicious?"

"I shouldn't say." Dickon leaned forwards over the table and lowered his voice to the point that Rosie could hardly hear him. "You really mustn't tell this to anyone else. But Master Karp admitted he was out on the night of the murder, but he refused to tell me where he'd gone. He said it was a private matter. So immediately I smelled the clue."

"Ah, interesting," said Rosie, guessing Mandrake had probably been out flying, and could hardly say so. "But it's not actual proof, is it."

Their supper was carried out to them, and since it looked and smelled delicious, they stopped talking in order to eat. Rosie's mouth was stuffed with roast lamb, when, looking up, she saw Mandrake himself entering the tavern, with Peg at his side. Rosie nearly choked on her lamb.

Peg walked over. "Well, well, what a delightful surprise," she said, pulling off the hood of her cloak. She still had the white blob of seagull dropping on the top of her head, attached to her equally white hair. It looked almost intentional.

"I was discussing the weather with the sheriff's assistant," Rosie said, attempting dignity. "And we were both – hungry."

"So am I. Starving," Peg grinned. "And I wanted to talk to Mandrake. But not about the weather." Without being invited, she sat beside Rosie, squashing up a bit since the table was tiny, and Mandrake squeezed in beside Dickon, which made him quite irritated.

"Hardly polite," he said.

"I forgive you," said Mandrake. "No need to apologise. Now, Master Wald, you're just the right person to ask. We want to know how your investigation is going."

Dicken swallowed his last slice of roast lamb and shook his head. "Out of the question," he said. "I cannot discuss such a matter with anyone except the sheriff. Utterly private. So no questions, please."

"I quite understand," said Mandrake. "I wouldn't dream of putting you in a difficult position. So what do you actually need as some sort of proof to arrest someone and put them up for trial?"

"Well," Dickon relented, "whatever seems convincing. Knowing he did it. If they confess, of course, and you can wallop them a bit to encourage a confession."

"I thought the new king was against that sort of corruption," interrupted Peg.

"That's not corruption," Dickon frowned. "It's common sense. Very few folk will confess without encouragement. And if we already know they did it, whatever it is, then that's fair enough."

"So tell me," continued Mandrake, "how can you tell *when* someone was killed if no one saw it happen."

"Very simple," Dickon sniffed. "If someone was seen alive at midday, as an example, and did not come home again even at supper time, then they were killed sometime between midday and supper time."

Everybody stared at everybody else. "Fascinating," smiled Peg with a faint gulp. "And forgive me for changing the subject, but what do you and the sheriff generally think of The Rookery? We believe we are a very quiet and law-abiding home for old people, who would have trouble looking after themselves, including me, of course. And we never interfere with village business. So is that how you see us too? As law abiding citizens? No complaints, for instance?"

"Oh, gracious indeed," Dickon hurried to answer, and gulped down his ale, "never a complaint, mistress. The village people see The Rookery as a home of great generosity. To open a place where old folk can live peacefully, and be cared for until the inevitable end, is a very moral idea, mistress. The sheriff and I approve." He finished the last slurp of ale. "Until, of course," he said as an afterthought, "a rather nasty murder takes place on the premises."

"Naturally," smiled Mandrake. "And of course we value your interest in that particular shocking affair. Got any clues?"

"Someone from the same home, I suppose," Dickon mumbled. "But no special ideas, sadly. Old folk aren't usually strong enough to do so much damage. Perhaps it could have been a witch."

Everyone again stared, heads jerking up from their cups.

"A witch?"

"I'm not serious, of course." Dickon smiled. "That was a joke. We all know there aren't any witches or wizards around here."

Three gentle sighs answered him.

"But you may remember," Rosie said softly, "when you first visited The Rookery, it was because people had complained about the smell from the murdered man's corpse. So people did complain."

"Well, yes, indeed," huffed Dickon. "But a very understandable problem, you know, considering that smell. Folk walking by, you see. But I myself am quite grateful, since it brought me to your home and has introduced you to me." He gazed at Rosie with wide-eyed appreciation.

"You're grateful someone got murdered?" asked Peg, managing a very sober voice.

"Oh, no, no, no, no," hiccupped Dickon, but Rosie patted his arm, assuring him they all understood.

It was soon after that Dickon put down his cup and pushed back his stool, smiling at Rosie. "Well, mistress," he said, "I think it's time I saw you back home."

"Oh no, don't worry," grinned Rosie. "Peg and Mandrake will see me back. We all live in the same house, as you know."

"But—" managed Dickon.

Peg shook her head. "We shan't be here long, Master Wald," she said. "It would make no sense for you to walk all that way when we shall be right behind you."

"And I shall be there in the middle," Mandrake added, "ready to protect the ladies should we meet up with a witch or wizard."

With a highly disappointed smile, Dickon nodded, said goodbye with a particular little wave at Rosie and wandered out of the tavern into the outside twilight. Immediately Rosie flopped back against the wall, Peg flopped forwards against the table, and Mandrake smirked.

"Well, no need to worry about him," he said softly.

"The man is a complete idiot," exclaimed Peg, turning to Rosie. "Typical human. And you actually left The Rookery with him to come here. Why on earth did you do that?"

"Because my mother's supper smelled disgusting," confessed Rosie. "And besides, I wanted to know if he'd found out anything of importance."

"He'd not notice it, even if someone told him in detail that he'd done it," said Mandrake. "I doubt the boy has any more brain than Cabbage."

"I'll have you know that Cabbage is quite bright," complained Peg. "But you're right. We'll get no useful information out of that idiot."

"But it *was* useful," Rosie pointed out. "Now we know he hasn't any idea about anything."

"Which is why we followed you," Mandrake said. "We wanted to check him out."

Rosie scowled and continued, "And it's equally clear that Little Piddleton thinks we are just lovely old people in need of care."

"In need of wine," Peg contradicted her. "Let's have a decent drink, and then we can fly home."

CHAPTER TEN

Three crows sat at the end of Rosie's bed. She woke and blinked. "Gracious," she muttered, "am I that late?"

"We aren't an alarm clock," one crow objected. "This is a personal visit. May I introduce myself? I am Wolfy, and this is my partner Cuddles. "

"I'm Lucky," said the third Crow. "I wanted to come too. This is my mum and dad."

"We couldn't get rid of her," Wolfy explained. "But we came for a very specific reason."

"I even left little Wobbles and Fips and Jolly and Tiger behind in their nest," said Cuddles. "No one's even sitting on them, let alone feeding them. They'll be squawking their little bony heads off. We have to hurry back with a few strips of something or other. So we have to be quick."

Lucky was looking very pleased with herself. "I'm the grown-up daughter," she said proudly. "I help with the new little brats. They've all broken out of their shells now, and just think of food, food, food. I like Fips best. She makes a racket like the others, but at least she says thank you once she's swallowed everything."

"What's so urgent?" Rosie pulled the sheet up under her chin. "I might have a few strips of something myself under the bed, if you hop down and have a look. The bread was so over baked for yesterday's breakfast, I stuffed it away. Help yourselves."

Wolfy and Cuddles sent Lucky to hop beneath and find it while they spoke of other matters.

As she watched, Rosie asked, "Do you know how Splodge is getting on? My father was looking after him. Or her. I can't tell the difference at that age."

"Her," said Cuddles, "and she's getting on very well. I won't say your father makes a very realistic crow, but he's a good father."

"I know," Rosie sighed.

"We were especially friendly with poor Whistle," Wolfy said. "Not only do we miss him dreadfully, but we hoped to find some of his special belongings. Useful stuff, you know. Not money or boring things like that. But a bit of helpful magic."

"Did you want a reminder? A souvenir? Then you don't want me," Rosie pointed out. "It was Kate who cleaned the room. By the time I went back in there, nothing of Whistle's was left." Then she thought of what Peg had bought from Kate. "However," she admitted, "there are two of Whistle's magical belongings Peg got from Kate, and paid too, so I can't give them to you. I can only tell you about them. Anything else important, I'd bet my mother has it."

"But I believe that you have – ?" asked Cuddles.

"A silver spoon, too large for a proper spoon," Rosie admitted, without the slightest intention of showing these items, "and a sort of pretend silver toadstool. Just a little thing with silver dots etched on it. But they aren't mine, so I can't give them to you."

Lucky hopped back up with three long curly crusts in her beak. Wolfy nodded to Rosie. "We have no wish to take the silver from you," he said. "But we think we should warn you. These, and a few others, of Whistle's special and precious invented items should not be used unknowingly. They could be – "

"Dangerous," finished Cuddles. "Especially that nuisance of a toadstool. Put it in a box and leave it somewhere hidden."

"Why?" Frowning, Rosie leaned back on the pillows. The silver objects were strange enough to have been used for something, and Whistle was powerful enough to have invented objects for a special purpose. Those items had certainly not been purely decoration, so the crow's words did not surprise her. Yet when she had briefly examined them, nothing interesting had occurred. She said, "But Whistle wasn't a dark wizard. He was kind and helpful. I even remember him coming to my power test when I was ten."

"Well, he would have, wouldn't he?" demanded Wolfy.

Cuddles hopped closer, and her voice was unusually soft. "We are trying to help, you know," she said with a faint clack of her beak. "We knew Whistle well, and we want to help. Please just remember our words."

This startled Rosie even more, and she sensed something almost frightening at the back of the unusual warning. So she sat up and faced all three crows. "Thank you for coming," she said, smiling wide. She decided she couldn't hug them, in spite of Cuddles' name, but she added, "I suppose you don't have any idea who did this horrible thing to Whistle?"

But they shook their heads, preparing to fly off with her stale crusts. But Wolfy waited on the window sill, and turned, whispering, "Whistle had a particular interest in you, Mistress Rosie, and so do we. If anything bad happens, you just let us know. And in the meantime, if you could find Whistle's silver cup, larger than your average ale cup, of course, it might solve some mysteries."

Rosie was left perturbed, filled with curiosity and just a little scared. She didn't understand how anyone, especially anyone as clever as Whistle, could possibly have had any special interest in her, and with the crows, it seemed plain ridiculous. Her mind whizzed. Knowing herself to be an ordinary fifty, none of this extra attention made any sense at all.

Once up and dressed, Rosie hurried downstairs for her usual jobs, making the beds, three heavy buckets of water and setting the table for breakfast. On the verge of arriving late, her mother glared in disapproval, and Rosie knew she'd have to avoid her for the rest of the day, or she'd end up being ordered to scrub floors, wash windows and dust every corner. Dusting was an especially hard job at The Rookery as it was important not to injure any of the resident spiders, and try not to ruin all their webs.

For today, Rosie had very different ideas, and once she'd finished her breakfast she ran straight back to her bedchamber and retrieved the silver toadstool and large spoon from their hiding places. She was already wearing the ruby hatpin, and hoped the entire and interesting collection would give answers.

A little wooden table sat in the corner of her bedchamber, and she sat next to this, laying out the two silver objects in front of her, and then waking hatpin Oswald with a gentle rub.

"Please," said Rosie aloud, "I'm feeling a little titchy bit upset. Odd things keep happening to me. I thought I was being good wanting to find who killed Whistle. Mostly because it was terrible and wicked, but also because I liked Whistle. I didn't expect easy answers, but I would greatly appreciate it if any of you could explain what's going on."

"Feeling sorry for yourself, girl?" demanded the toadstool, and its spots glimmered gold.

"Perhaps I am." Rosie was cross. "But it's Whistle I'm trying to help. Well, it's a bit late for that, but you know what I mean."

"I've no idea what you mean," said the toadstool. "I don't even know who you are. I only ever speak to Whistle himself, and I prefer it when he's in a good mood."

It was the spoon which interrupted, speaking more genially. "Now, now," it said, flashing blue across its large silver scoop. "I know you miss our master, and so do I. But this is the girl. Remember?"

"Rosie?" boomed the toadstool.

"Keep your voices down," objected Oswald from Rosie's collar. "Say what you can, and say it softly."

It seemed the toadstool was now rather ashamed of itself. "Rosie," it muttered. "Mistress Rosie herself. Well now, I apologise. But it isn't my fault, you know. I can't see. No eyes, all my spots are ears."

"I have both," said the spoon with a superior air. "My scoop is my eye, and I have ears up the handle. And, I may say, I am a generous and giving spoon. I can give when directed. I bestow, and that is my name, Mistress Rosie. I am Bestower Brim."

"How do you do," said Rosie, wide-eyed.

"I'm just as important," insisted the toadstool. "I take, but only where there's too much. What I take, I give to Bestower, and then he can give it to someone else. And I am Mush Mutter, although I dislike being thought of as a mushroom. How do you do, Mistress Rosie."

"How do you do." She couldn't imagine what to ask. Taking and giving were vague talents and made very little sense. "But what did Whistle ask you to give or take away?"

"This and that."

"Hard to explain," added Mush.

So Rosie asked Oswald. "I wonder if you can tell me more? What am I supposed to do now? And who on earth killed poor Whistle?"

This had not been a wise question, since the hat pin, the spoon and the toadstool all burst into tears. Rosie sighed and packed the silver objects safely away, deciding to search for the silver cup, as advised by the crows. There were only two places she could think of, and one was the kitchen where she didn't want to go. Instead she hurried up all the stairs to Whistle's two large rooms. With Peg living close by, Rosie was quiet. She decided she had to avoid both Peg and her mother. For once, she felt the freedom to do exactly as she wished, and stop everyone going on about her, instead of concentrating on Whistle.

Although Alice had decided not to advertise these rooms yet for occupation, they had been sufficiently tidied to making finding a single thing most unlikely. Both large, the rooms would bring in excellent rent for her parents, and Alice intended on taking two more lodgers, with one bedchamber each.

"Twice the money. And just think, two more friends," Alice had said, though she had not really made friends with a single occupant so far.

So Rosie scurried inside and began a flurried search on her knees. There was nothing under the bed, nothing under any stool or chair, nothing under the two tables and not a single item left on any shelf. Rosie looked on the window sill, on the candle sconces, lifted the squashy cushions on the chair and even lifted up the three Turkey rugs. She found nothing. Her knees ached from crawling, and her back ached from bending.

Finally, Rosie stood, yawned and prepared to leave, when a very high-pitched voice squeaked out, "What about me?" Rigid, Rosie looked around. "Over here," squeaked the voice. "I've been hiding for ages. It's most uncomfortable."

Tracing the call, Rosie rushed to the bed and rummaged beneath the eiderdown at one side, where everything was tucked tight. There she was able to pull out a somewhat crumpled piece of parchment. "Gosh," she said, "you actually hid? How clever. Are you important?"

"Important? I'm jolly well essential," said the parchment, insulted. "Now, roll me up carefully and put me in your apron pocket."

"I don't suppose," asked Rosie hopefully, "you know where the silver cup is? I was told that's terribly important too."

"Alice Scaramouch," said the parchment. "I'd guess it has to be her. Probably has taken it and uses it for her evening wine. It won't poison her, but you have to get it back."

"That won't be easy," Rosie mumbled, did as asked with the parchment and hurried from the room. On her way back down the stairs, Oswald stuck his pin into her chin, and Rosie almost tripped. "What? Have I left something behind?"

"Loads," scolded Oswald. "A quill pen and invisible ink under the pillows. A pair of shoes that take you flying when you're too tired to do it for yourself. They're on a top shelf at the back, so high you can't see them. And…"

But just as Rosie was about to object and ask Oswald why he hadn't told her all this when she was inside the two rooms, she bumped into Peg. It seemed that Peg was about to object as well.

"I've been looking for you all morning," said Peg. "I spoke to Kate again and offered more bribes. Coin, a warm cloak – that sort of thing. She's promised to tell me what she can remember finding in Whistle's rooms, whatever she kept and whatever she knows your mother kept."

"We asked her all that before," said Rosie.

"A little extra bribery goes a long way," said Peg. "And she's a poor little thing. Only a twelve. Can barely click her fingers." She thought for a moment. "Mind you, that's probably because she uses them all the time for picking her nose."

"Oh dear, alright," Rosie sighed. "I suppose I ought to tell you, I went back to search Whistle's room one last time, and I found a piece of paper who insists she's important."

"Show me," said Peg at once. As Rosie pulled the parchment from her apron, Peg snatched it and began to read. Her face lit with purple anticipation, and finally she beamed. Having rolled it once more, she then handed it back to Rosie. "Keep this very, very safe," she said. "I can explain when we find a few more things. In the meantime, don't show a soul. Keep it hidden."

"I don't have so many special places for keeping stuff hidden," Rosie complained. "My room is only a single. Wouldn't you like to hide these things instead of me?"

Peg waved both hands at her. "No, no, my dear. It's you they all want to stay with. Shoved in my room, they'd start running around and making nuisances of themselves."

"I spend half my life absolutely puzzled," Rosie objected.

"Number one, puzzled, confused, muddled and not understanding. Number two, a big quarter I spend scared."

"And the last quarter?"

"Number three, working my knees raw and my back broken." Rosie sat where she was at the top of the old staircase. "You're understanding more than I am. Won't you start explaining at least some of it?"

Peg hovered mid-air, just above the lower steps. "I understand bits here and bits there, and being a most powerful witch, I know the river is starting to flow. But I'm afraid I could never explain it to you, Rosie dear."

"Because at just fifty, I'm too stupid to understand?"

"As it happens," smiled Peg, "I don't think you are a fifty at all, my dearest. But that's something else I can't explain."

"Oh, pooh," said Rosie. "I can't fly. I can't polish things with a click of my fingers. I can't understand magic runes, like those on this parchment, and I can't do any special spells. No disguises, no curses, no blessings and not even good dreams on call."

"You flew right up into the clouds, and stayed there," Peg pointed out. "That day on the beach proved what you're capable of. And how do you wash and get dressed every morning?"

"Well, that's simple. Everyone can do that," Rosie said. "I can click my fingers for some little things. But nothing big."

"We shall see," Peg told her.

It was as Rosie clattered downstairs, with Peg flying above, that she thought of something and asked, "Why were you out with Mandrake yesterday? I've never liked Mandrake. But you seemed happy with him."

"Yes," Peg sighed. "You like Montague, because he's good looking and seems a whole lot younger than he really is. But Montague can't even remember your name and hardly knows you exist. Mandrake, on the other hand, likes me."

Immediately disinterested, Rosie changed the subject. "I thought about the bats too," she said. "They fly at night, and Whistle was murdered at night. They just could have seen someone. But I doubt I'd understand them, and probably they wouldn't want to talk to me. But they like you too, you said, and you get on well together. So have you asked the bats if they saw anything that night?"

"A highly sensible idea," Peg agreed. "We shall go together tonight after supper. But had they seen anything horrible, I'm sure they'd have told me already." She shrugged. "You never know. We'll take some wine and biscuits, and go to the attic tonight for a bat chat."

CHAPTER ELEVEN

Understanding each other after all, the bats seemed very pleased to see Rosie. Rosie was distinctly surprised and equally delighted. One small bundle of soft fur upended itself so its head actually cuddled into Rosie's hair.

"You smell so nice," it told her. "Sort of familiar. Welcome to our belfry."

"But no bell," muttered Rosie, not entirely sure she wanted a bat, however friendly, feeling cheerfully at home in her hair.

Peg sat just as cheerfully on the piles of guano, looking perfectly content. It was hard to see if the bats were smiling, but a huge number flapped down onto beams closer to their visitors.

"Whistle's window?" answered one. "No. I never fly close in case I disturb him. Such a nice and clever man."

"Didn't you know he was dead?" Rosie was surprised.

"I did," several called from the beams.

And one said, "I knew, poor gennleman. And I seen summit too."

Eagerly leaning forwards, Rosie asked, "What? Can you describe what you saw?"

"He were lyin' proper dead," answered the bat. "All smashed and squashed, he were, and I seen the door shuttin' an' all."

"So who left the room?" Now Peg was equally excited.

"Dunno," said the bat. "I only seen a foot goin' out in a boot, it were. A boring brown boot."

Immediately Rosie and Peg started to think who wore brown boots. "One, sometimes me," started Rosie. "Number two, Mandrake. He did last night."

"And me, and everyone," Peg objected, and looked up again at the bat. "Large? Small? Insignificant? Dirty? Polished? Buckle or laces or ribbons?"

"Oh, botheration," said the bat, and paused to think. "Reckon they was big. Reckon they was an itchy bit grubby. No polish. Laces, it were. Just a dirty old brown cord tyin' up a brown boot."

"Now that," grinned Peg, "is extremely useful."

As gently as possible, Rosie dislodged the bat's little head from her hair. "I'm sure I shall see you again," she said. "I'm Rosie."

"Oooo, I knows," whispered the bat into her ear. "And you smells proper sweet. I's Milly, and I reckons I shall see you again."

For the entire remainder of the evening, without realising there were large patches of guano stuck to the backs of their gowns, Rosie and Peg tottered around The Rookery staring at everyone's feet.

This did not go unnoticed.

It was eventually Montague who said loudly, "Mistress Tipple, you seem remarkably interested in my shoes. Yes, they are pointed, and emerald green leather with an extremely attractive copper buckle. Is this of the slightest importance to you?"

Looking up, Peg said, "Do you have any brown boots, perhaps?"

"You wish to borrow my boots, madam?" He pointed to her feet. "Yes, I have very smart brown boots tied in a handsome red ribbon. But I must point out that your feet are considerably smaller than mine. You would fall top over tail."

She shook her head. "Just wondering. Taste and fashion, you know."

Montague gazed back. "Since I disbelieve you, madam," he said with considerable hauteur, "I suggest we all convene in the meeting hall tomorrow morning immediately after breakfast. Get that old turnip Alice too, and her silly little daughter. But I doubt the maid or the gardener would be of any use. And you can proceed to carry out your own interrogation, using fire tongs and red-hot pokers, if you wish, to discover our footwear and work out who you think killed Master Hobb."

Rosie blushed, and Peg smiled. "Excellent. I do believe the time has come. It's precisely what I planned myself. So ring the kitchen bell, and tell everyone the moment of disclosure will come in the morning."

Now late April, the sunshine was strong and enjoyed peeping into every window each morning. Breakfast had been served and eaten, and they had gathered in the main hall.

It was quite a squash. Even without Rosie's father, Alfred, the maid, Kate, and the gardener, there were thirteen witches and ten wizards. Montague suggested they sit in order of merit, according to their magical power, but others shouted him down.

"Just because you think you're special at seventy-one."

"Whereas *I'M* a seventy-eight," said Mandrake with a large smile.

"Sit wherever you wish," Peg shouted at them. "And let's get on with this before midday dinner."

"If I am kept here," Alice sniffed, "dinner will be late."

"Then we could all go down to the Juggler and Goat," beamed Rosie, but no one took any notice.

Montague and Mandrake pulled up their stools but sat on opposite sides of the room. Alice did not sit next to her daughter and glared at Peg. Emmeline, a stout seventy-two, sat next to Rosie and gazed placidly while sucking her chocolate, which wouldn't be discovered until many, many years later, and Emmeline's was nicer anyway. Next to her sat Butterfield Short, a full seventy-nine. Leaving a polite space between, Pixie West sat, almost equal at seventy-six. Taking the vacancy between them, Bertie Cackle, an eighty-two in grubby brown boots, sat himself down and stretched out his legs. Apart from Peg, he was now the most powerful wizard there.

Gradually, each wizard and each witch took their places, staring with interest at each other. It was extremely rare that all The Rookery inhabitants agreed to meet together.

"It's not just astrology," announced Ermengarde Spank, a tidy sixty-four. "One of our most interesting and powerful neighbours has been murdered in shocking circumstances. We should have discovered the perpetrator before now."

"I quite like astrology," muttered Gorgeous Leek, who was only a nineteen and so never wanted to be noticed.

"I," said Montague, "have no interest in the matter. Whistle Hobb was a fool who played with spoons and candle sticks, and wrote books that William Caxton refused to print."

Lemony Limehouse often behaved with surprising levity, but everyone knew beneath the giggles, she was a respectable sixty-six. "I do believe,' she said, "we were all in our beds at that time. No one heard anything, and no one saw anything. Except the killer, of course. So how do we find out?"

"What about asking the bats?"

"Done."

"What about the crows?"

"Done."

"What about the owls?

Rosie looked up. "I haven't spoken to Rocky. I did with Cabbage, but I forgot Rocky. Of all those who could have seen what went on at night, Rocky might be the most appropriate."

"Then stop bothering the rest of us," said Montague.

Rosie went off him in an instant. "But we ought to continue talking here and now," she said. "There's a lot to learn. For instance, did anyone hear footsteps?"

Montague sighed. "As a fifty you may have to walk," he said. "But most of us more talented wiccans choose to fly."

Rosie snapped her mouth shut and left the rest to Peg.

Boris, short stocky and a somewhat tough little twenty-four, sat back behind most of the others and muttered, "Humbug. Pissywallop. Pendigo-parcels. Squirrel breath and toppsy-turvey-pickled rodents and hedgehogs swimming swamps."

"There are certain facts which I see as obvious," Peg said, ignoring Boris. "As such a powerful wizard, Whistle can only have been killed by someone over a seventy. For that sort of physical strength as well as magical power, it has to have been a male. He may have entered by the window, but he left by the door, so he walked some of the way." Here she scowled at Montague. "He wore brown boots on large feet. And he didn't like Whistle."

"That means almost everyone," Alice interrupted, standing with an impatient sniff. "And since it excludes me, I'm going to the kitchen to start dinner, and Rosie can come and help."

But Peg shook her head. "Rosie has been investigating this situation from the start. She needs to stay here."

Alice flounced off alone, and Rosie looked around as more than half The Rookery occupants were pushing over their stools, ready to leave. "But," she called, "someone could have seen something, even if they didn't do it themselves."

It was Percy Rotten who marched to Peg, raising his voice. "OK. I'm a sixty-nine, not strong, but enough when something matters. I could have killed the wretched man, since I never liked him. I'm strong in both ways, and I own a great pair of brown boots which I never bother to polish. My feet are definitely large. So it could have been me. But it wasn't. Why would I bother? There's lots of people here I don't like, including you, Madam Tipple. But I'm not going to trot around killing anyone who annoys me. And how could you prove it anyway, even if I did?"

"Besides," said Mandrake, "if any of us disliked someone enough to bounce them off in such a manner, why wait until now? If I'd wanted to, I'd have done something years back."

"Squeezy – wheezy. Spooky – slosh. What a dipsy waste of time," muttered Boris. "Teezle-weezle and pintified bricks."

"I'm inclined to agree with Boris," said Mandrake, leaning back with a yawn.

Rosie was disappointed, but smiled at Peg and wandered out to join her mother. "It's obvious we're getting nowhere. I suppose I'd better go and help my miserable mother."

It was on her way to the kitchen that she bumped into Uta Hampton, the impressive eighty-one who rarely spoke to anyone. "I was wondering," she said softly, "whether Whistle was working on anything new lately." Smiling, she pulled Rosie into a shadowed corner. "It's probably finding the motive that is so interesting, you know," she said. "The why, and the why now? All sorts of us might have had the occasional conversation, you know, giving some faint disclosure of what he was doing. Only motive will unmask our villain."

Rosie supposed this was true. "And you were friendly with him," she smiled back. "Have you any idea?"

"Unfortunately not," she murmured. "He disliked discussing his work, as most of us do. But it's possible he was discovering some facts that disproved someone else's work, made another of us look foolish, or simply proved their work false. Mandrake or Montague, for instance, since they both fancy themselves magical geniuses. I'd believe both of them capable of killing someone who threatened to make them look like the idiots they are."

"So both capable of bashing an old man's head in." Rosie gulped. "Just to keep him quiet."

"True." Uta nodded. "But I confess, I'm less interested in finding the guilty one. After all, we must die eventually, every one of us. Sometimes such long lives prove most tedious. Whistle had led a remarkably interesting two hundred years. Perhaps that's enough."

Rosie, however, knew nothing of any wizard's present work, since her only job usually involved sweeping, dusting and scrubbing. She thanked Uta and plodded to the kitchen. She had insisted on leaving the one secret paper she had found in Whistle's room with Peg and hoped that might bring up new ideas. Peg, for all her muddles, was an expert at the wiccan runes. But since the room had originally held at least a thousand papers of all kinds, the discovery of one was unlikely to prove significant. The other nine hundred and ninety-nine had evidently been destroyed.

Watching her mother boiling a watery gravy in the cauldron over the fire, and since it was still hot outside, Rosie spoke from the doorway. "You don't really need me, do you, Mamma?"

Alice snorted. "Why should I ever actually need you, girl?" She returned to the stirring. "Once this is hot enough, I shall turn it into mutton and peas. "I might add a little chutney on the side. And parsnip jelly for pudding."

"Must it be parsnip jelly? What about blackberry jelly?"

Alice didn't bother turning around. "I shall make whatever I wish, rude brat. You can go and play."

"I was just wondering," wondered Rosie, "how you can turn hot water into proper dinner. You're a fifty like me. I can't do things like that, and I can't even fly. Couldn't you have taught me a thing or two?"

Her mother snorted back over her shoulder. "I've taught you a thing and ten," she said without turning. "Obedience, cleaning up, keeping out of my way. That's enough for me."

Biting her lip and refusing to get annoyed, Rosie asked, "Whistle's papers? There were so many, and they might have held clues. But Kate says you had them all torn up and set on fire."

"Naturally," Alice bothered to answer. "I could hardly leave a mess like that for our new lodger. And I might add she's arriving tomorrow. She'll pay a high rent, since she wants both rooms, and I shall greet her myself when she flies in."

"Do you know her number?" Not that it mattered.

"Oh yes indeed," replied Alice. "She's a nice warm ninety-three."

Rosie gasped. "Ninety-three? That's nearly the whole hundred. Have you met her yet? Is she nice? Do you know her name?"

"Twenty-five questions as always," sighed her mother. "Yes, yes, yes, and yes. There's just one no, since I haven't met her yet. But she's flying down from the north. I believe she's been living in a cave in the Scottish mountains. An odd choice, but I suppose as a ninety-three she can keep herself warm wherever she is."

"And she's arriving tomorrow?" Rosie was quite excited at such a powerful new-comer. Even Whistle had only been a ninety-one.

CHAPTER TWELVE

Sitting at her own little table which she used as a desk, Peg stretched out Whistle's last surviving piece of parchment, which Rosie had left with her, and attempted to decipher the codes and scattered runes. This was no beautiful illuminated manuscript, and no gorgeous pictures nor decorated letters adorned it. There simply seemed to be a mess of scribble. Yet Peg was magical enough herself to know that this was surely a disguise, and a disguise was only ever used to hide something important.

"Emphatic," she read out, using her fingers constantly just in case something turned out to be a spell. "Sing at the sun. Spoon up the negatives and pour the positives into the cup." Mentions of spoons and cups interested her since both those items had been spoken of as relevant. Rosie kept the spoon safe in her room, but no one had yet discovered the cup. "But that greedy old baggage won't have chucked it," Peg muttered, "since it was silver." She read on. "One, two – three – four – humph," she said. "Sounds like Rosie."

Yet half the signs were unreadable even to her, and she leaned back, gazed from the window and sank into dreams.

Rosie rushed in, wishing Peg a good morning. and skipped to

her side. "Edna Edith Ethel Enid Elsie Oppolox is our new resident," she said, "she's coming today, and she's a ninety-three."

Peg refused to appear impressed. "Then I hope she doesn't show it off," she said. "In the meantime, I'm trying to understand this wretched parchment of Whistle's."

"Perhaps Edna will be able to," Rosie suggested.

"You mean perhaps we should give it to Edna whatever her name is when she arrives?"

"I just meant, if you were tired of it—"

"Certainly not," grunted Peg. "As soon as the poor woman arrives, you think we should tell her she's taken over the rooms of someone recently murdered, and would you please read this parchment before hanging your cloak up?"

"Alright," Rosie nodded, accustomed to being told off. "Besides, it's quite easy, isn't it? I expect you read it ages ago. I mean, the spoon and the cup. And that's the same number of spots as the toadstool," she said, pointing to where the dots were. "Here's the wind whistling down the chimney, so he means himself. This could be a Rosie rose, but I'm quite sure he isn't writing about me. And that's multiplication, with a hand, and an umbrella. In the end, there's a sliver of papers like glass shards, glass being transparent, so papers easy to read. And I think it means go and stand in the rain with the cup, the spoon and the toadstool, and demand the return of anything you've lost or been destroyed."

Peg stared at her young friend in absolute amazement. "How on earth did you manage that?"

"I may be a fifty, but I'm not an idiot," sniffed Rosie.

Having worked on that parchment for two days without being able to read it, Peg was somewhat shocked. "True," she said in a mumbled undertone. "Well done, dear. Then this could be exactly what we need to do. Wait for the rain, and we can demand the return of all those papers your mother destroyed. And it will take us weeks, but we can study every one of them and find the clue to the murderer."

"I'm looking forward to meeting this new witch," Rosie said. "She's been living in a cave. But a ninety-three? Gosh. That's special."

"Not much more than an eighty-six."

Rosie got the point. "Almost the same," she agreed. "But a new look from an outsider – you know – can be useful."

It wasn't raining. They looked at each other. "I shall see if I can summon up a little drizzle," Peg decided.

"Alright." Rosie sighed. "I suppose I should go and search for the silver cup. But if Mother has it, and I go hunting amongst her precious belongings, she'll carve me into crumbs."

"Get someone down there to call her out for a long, concentrated task," Peg suggested, "to keep her out of the way. Then sneak in. You always make her bed anyway, don't you?"

"I did that already."

"Well, do it again."

Since she wasn't offering to call Alice away herself, Rosie accepted she was being dismissed, and trotted all the way down the endless staircase to the ground floor, and went to find a friendly soul who would call her mother out of the way. She was wandering the corridors when the front door whooshed open, and a tall thin woman, struggling with a huge feathered hat, a long velvet cloak that seemed determined to entangle itself, three large baskets of belongings, the rattan baskets painted with flowers, and a big fat white bird on her shoulder which seemed nervous and was demanding comfort by pecking the woman's ear, entered in a flap and flurry, almost sinking to the floor once she arrived indoors.

She saw Rosie, who had run to help with the luggage. "Oh, my dear girl, thank you," said the woman. "I should have flown, but I was worried that someone might see me. Of course I didn't know how your beautiful old house was situated. Had it been in the middle of a town, I couldn't have dived down the chimney."

Rosie was excited. "You're the new ninety-three," she said, hauling up the baskets but keeping a distance from the parrot.

"Welcome to The Rookery. My mother owns the place, and I'm Rosie."

"My dear Rosie," Edna said at once, "I'm delighted to be here, and I'm delighted to meet you. Perhaps you'll point me in the right direction?"

Pointing dutifully, Rosie said, "Top floor. Rooms One and Two. It says so on the doors. You can fly straight up, but I'll tell my mother, and she'll follow up to greet you and talk about breakfast and dinner and other stuff." She had thought of the perfect solution. "I'm sure you'll want to talk to her at some length. I shall be thrilled to meet you later at supper."

Clutching the handles of all three baskets flicking her cloak out of the way and threatening the bird with decapitation unless it stopped eating her ear, the woman disappeared up into the long dark stairwell, feet clicking toes together as she disappeared.

With another happy skip, Rosie ran to the kitchen. "Mamma, she's arrived. I mean, Edna Oppolox. She's delightful but she has a funny bird. White. No, not a pigeon, I mean a real white white, and I've never seen such a white bird before. I doubt it will get on well with the ravens, but that's their problem. I've directed her to her rooms, but she says she wants a lovely long conversation with you, to help her settle in and get to know everything."

"I suppose so." Alice sighed. "And plenty of time before supper. But the high numbers can be very arrogant, like Whistle."

"She didn't seem arrogant."

Heaving herself from the chair, Alice staggered from the kitchen, grabbed her skirts and flew upstairs. Rosie quickly slipped from the kitchen door, along the outside passage and into her mother's spacious apartment.

Rummaging without leaving a trace proved hard work, and Rosie worried a little that her mother might simply use magic to discover who had been in her rooms. But since her mother's magic was no better than hers, she felt a bit safer and kept looking. She was somewhat surprised to discover four large wooden chests under the large covered bed, which she had tidied herself that morning. But she had never looked beneath before. Now she pulled out the first chest. It was locked with both padlock and spell, and Rosie thought she had no chance of breaking in, but tried anyway. She'd heard spells like this before and knew just two simple answers.

She said, "I summon this lock to break with a plop, and whatever is spoken, let it be open. So – OPEN." She'd been taught that as a child and did not expect good results. And yet, with the requested plop, the padlock fell open, and the chest's heavy wooden lid swept upwards all on its own.

Rosie stared. It was stuffed full with a thousand papers or more, and she recognised some as having been Whistle's. So her mother had not torn or burned the magic papers at all, she had smuggled them away and burned something entirely different to look as if she had. Rosie pushed the lid back down and pulled out the next chest.

This had two padlocks, and Rosie spoke the same spell but without success.

"Bother," she mumbled. "What was the other one I used to know? Oh yes, a bit too simple, but let's try. Hubble, bubble, toil and trumble, kick the lock and make it crumble."

She aimed and kicked. The chest flipped open its lid with a jerk, and Rosie stared inside with even more astonishment than she had with the previous one. This chest was gleamingly full to the brim with money, coins of every type from sovereigns and pennies to pounds and guineas. There was a ton of foreign coins with flashes of large silver tokens and big lumps of pure gold.

Gasping, finding it actually difficult to breathe, Rosie stared at this enormous and unexplained wealth. She supposed that the rent from twenty-one paying guests, with only two simple minded staff to pay out, would give her a reasonable savings chest. But this was more than seemed reasonable, even over two hundred years. Unless, of course, she had created some by magic, which meant they would fade away after a couple of days once removed from their companions.

With a gulp of utter fear, Rosie removed three coins, one pound each, and a solitary silver token. She couldn't drop them into her apron pocket in case they jangled, so she wrapped them in her kerchief and stuffed the parcel in her garter at the top of her stocking. Very carefully she closed the chest and pushed it back into place. If the coins faded after a few days, then she had no problem. And surely, stealing from one's mother wasn't the same as stealing from someone else.

Pulling out the next chest, Rosie discovered the problem, since she did not know a third spell of openings. "Just please open," she said, pleadingly and with both hands raised. To her absolute amazement, the chest slid open. It contained her mother's clothes. Rosie grinned. Presumably there had been no spell binding it in the first place.

So to the last chest, but this one refused to open. Rosie tried to pick the lock with her pen knife. She begged, kicked, thumped and pushed. Nothing opened. She said her two spells again, several times in fact, pleaded and demanded, and managed nothing at all. Eventually, having few options left, she returned to the first chest, opened it once more, retrieved a handful of papers to stuff into her apron pocket, closed and locked everything, and hurried from the room. She had searched nothing else, which made her feel a little pathetic, but she had already been too long and feared her mother's return. Besides, if she was going to hide anything, surely it would have been in one of those four chests. Whether a silver cup sat in the last chest, she could not know, but guessed it was.

Back in the kitchen, Rosie found it empty. Having no fondness for an empty kitchen, she first climbed the one storey to her own bedchamber and stuffed the stolen coins and parchments under her mattress, wishing she had magically locked chests of her own. Flopping back on her bed, she closed her eyes and tried to make sense of everything that had happened, and had certainly not made sense.

"Number One," she said, "my mother's a millionaire, which is ridiculous. She never gives me tuppence, if she can help it. Number two, she kept all Whistle's papers, even though she made a big scene of tearing them up and shoving them on the fire. Besides, she'd never understand most of them. Number three, does she ever talk to my father? Number four, who had the slightest motive to kill Whistle? Number five, who has the power to kill Whistle? The only witch or wizard I've ever known stronger than ninety-one, is this new arrival Edna. But she's only just turned up. She may be a whole ninety-three, but she can't turn time around."

Having almost sent herself to sleep with unanswered questions, Rosie jerked herself awake and sat up, heart pounding. Now she knew what she had to do next. So slipping from her room, she tiptoed downstairs, saw her mother snoozing in the kitchen, hurried past and went again to the back door.

Definitely no rain. The sun was shining with a sort of special gleam as if it knew something nobody else had realised. Rosie ran across the cobbled courtyard and aimed for the stables.

The stable building, once large enough for five or six horses, now made two cosy rooms, one for the maid and one for the gardener. The gardener's room echoed with sun bleached snores. Kate's room was quiet.

Having tapped quietly on the door several times without answer, Rosie then whispered through the gap by the door jam. "Kate, dear, no problem. Sleep on, if you like, and if you're there. I just wondered if you had any other bits of silver. You know what I mean. Even more importantly, do you have any of Whistle's papers? Do you know that my mother didn't destroy them after all, even though she pretended she did?"

After quite some time with no answer, Rosie knocked again. Then she whispered for a second time. "You might be out. I'll look in the main house. But I'll come back later."

Having felt a bit silly talking to an obviously empty room, Rosie walked back to the main house and trotted every storey in a brief search for the maid, who didn't seem to be anywhere. She had either gone shopping in the village, or was off on a pleasant walk beyond the trees. So Rosie sat herself in the meeting hall and waited for supper. She realised she had also been asleep, when the noise of introductions woke her. She opened her eyes to the swirling colours of every witch and every wizard meeting the new resident. The swirling of cloaks, pushing in and hurrying out, was the background to every tone of voice, including shouts and squeaks, shrill hellos and deeper goodbyes. There were lots of hugs, cheek kissing and hand clasping. Rosie stood up and joined in.

"Wonderful to meet such a powerful witch, Mistress Oppolox."

"Most impressive, madam. I do hope we get to talk at length soon."

"I believe I am the next in line, Mistress Edna, since I am an eighty-two. Not as high as a ninety-three of course, but next in line."

"No, you aren't, Bertie," said Peg, marching up to Edna. "How dedoo, Madam Edna? I'm an eighty-five, but still a good deal less than ninety-three. We used to have a ninety-one, but he left a few days ago. Nice to meet someone intelligent at last."

With a growing sense of familiar friendliness, Edna Oppolox clasped both Rosie's hands in greeting. "I feel we know each other already," Rosie said.

"Those are very pleasant words, Rosie, dear," Edna replied. "They hold a particular meaning."

"Really?" Puzzled again, Rosie smiled widely. There was unlikely to be much close understanding between a fifty and a ninety-three after all. But she liked the light squeeze of Edna's hand around her own.

Alice called over the buzzing of the crowd. "Rosie, go and fetch Kate. She must serve supper. I've made something very special to greet our new charming resident. Get her to meet me in the kitchen. You can come too, just don't drop anything."

Shrugging, Rosie smiled at Edna and trotted out into the courtyard once again, and across to the stables. Clearly Kate must be back in her room by now. Indeed, she should be in the kitchen ready to serve supper. Rosie again tapped on the door.

When there was no answer she banged and shouted. "Kate, I've been sent to fetch you. It's nearly supper time, and this is a special one."

There was still no answer. So with a very solid shoulder push, Rosie shoved open the door.

CHAPTER THIRTEEN

The body of the young girl lay on the floor, her blood soaking the small blue rug beneath her head. Her loose blonde hair was still sticky and dark, for both sides of her face had been smashed inwards.

Kate's body lay on its back, untouched except for the hands, still attached to the arms, but smashed into tiny pieces. Rosie stood a moment, her knees shaking, and her throat closed, refusing to breathe. It took her some moments, but eventually she tottered from the room and carefully closed the door behind her. Then she stumbled back to the meeting hall, and it was only afterwards that she realised she should have searched the room.

Instead she approached her mother. "Mamma, it's happened again."

"What has happened, foolish girl?" Alice was impatient and strode past her daughter into the kitchen. "I am extremely busy. Where's Kate?"

"That's the problem," Rosie said, easing into the revelation. "I'm very sorry to say that poor Kate is – dead."

Alice stared for a blink and then raised her voice in a tremulous shriek. "She's far too young to die. Where is she? What happened?"

Rosie started to explain, and then realised that as she staggered and trembled, she was actually being held up by Peg on one side and Edna on the other. "Can you face it again, my dear?" Peg whispered.

"I think so," Rosie whispered back, "as long as you're with me. I couldn't go alone."

"I shall be coming as well," Edna nodded. "My first day here is honoured by a mystery of horrible happenings. I can hardly ignore that."

Clearly Alice disliked the idea of her new important guest being involved in such a gory business, displeased even more than she was at losing her maid. But after opening her mouth to complain, she quickly shut it again. "Supper is nearly ready," she muttered with vague hope. "And it's a special one just for you."

"Oh, this won't take long," said Edna, and the three women hurried out to the stables.

Peg knelt, looking at the dead girl's smashed skull, while Edna bent over the other side. "Horribly brutal," Peg mumbled. "There are far simpler and cleaner ways of killing someone, especially for a wizard. Why use such extreme measures?"

"The act of someone with a dark twist," Edna said at once. "The act of killing may have many motives. But the method used is the choice of a wizard with a leaning to the dark side."

"We have none of those here," Peg insisted.

"Mm," mused Edna. "You might, without realising. Some wizards have a dark thread. And some darker wizards hide that side, ashamed of showing it, but are tempted to relieve themselves when they presume they will never be discovered."

"You mean," Rosie asked, "there might be no other reason to kill except for fun?"

"I believe we have a simple situation here," Peg insisted. "For there is just one obvious link between Whistle and Kate, and that's a few of Whistle's belongings which went missing after Kate cleaned his room for your arrival, Edna."

Edna muttered a few Celtic swear words under her breath. "I shall do what I can here," she said, still bending over the body, "and perhaps you two should search the room."

The small room was a mess, but it was not clear whether this signified an earlier search of the premises by the killer, or whether Kate always lived in an untidy muddle. But Peg groaned, "Nothing left, I'd wager. But I shall see what I can find." And Rosie began to search on the opposite side of the room.

The destruction of Kate's body still lay on the central rug when Rosie, Peg and Edna all stood together, admitting that nothing had been found. The room was now even more of a mess, but Peg sighed, "Not a thing, except her own dreary belongings, poor little thing."

And Rosie nodded. "I think she had some more of Whistle's silver. But either she hid it outside the room, or the killer took it."

"Unfortunately," Edna added, "I cannot get a grip on the killer. I sense both anger and pleasure, and I am fairly sure this was the work of a wizard, not some boring human."

"But a very powerful one," said Rosie, feeling sick again. "Because it must be the same one who killed Whistle, and he was too powerful to be killed so easily."

"Not necessarily." Edna sat back on her heels. "If this was one of your own familiar residents here, no one would expect an attack when a friendly face came to visit. I imagine your Whistle Hobb would have been taken by surprise just as this poor girl was, in her own room."

Both Rosie and Peg nodded earnestly. "I didn't think of that," said Rosie faintly.

Edna's hands hovered just over the body. "I cannot tell you who the killer is," she admitted. "But your maid certainly knew him. He was almost positively resident here and known to all of you. The meeting seems to have started with a friendly chat. But your maid may have attempted to defend herself when she realised what was coming, since her hands are also destroyed, possibly because she was trying to scratch her killer."

"Then," said Peg with a small clap, "we must look for any one of our wizards with scratches on his face or hands."

"Now that," agreed Rosie, "will be a wonderful clue. Almost proof."

"No wizard leaves easy proof," Peg reminded her. "A strong wizard – even an average one – can eliminate his own bruises and bangs."

It was a fine supper for those who knew nothing of the new murder, but since it had been planned for Edna, sadly she was the one who enjoyed it least. She, Peg and Rosie spent a great deal of time looking around the table to discover suspicious scratches on their companions, but eventually Edna thanked Alice for the magnificent feast, didn't mention that she hadn't enjoyed it and finally flew to the top floor and her own new apartment.

No one heard from her until the next morning. Meanwhile, Peg sat under the trees outside, listened to the squawking and screeching flurry of crows as they had their own supper and settled for sleep.

Avoiding the last few drops of birds' mess, Peg asked, "Now then. Who would have done such a thing?"

"Number one, someone who wants Whistle's latest secrets," Rosie said, "Two, he has scratches on face or wrists and hands. Three, he's got a really nasty side. Maybe he does horrible things in secret. Maybe he beats birds and cats. Four, he owns big brown boots and doesn't bother to clean them. Five, he lives here."

"At least we're getting a little further," Peg sighed.

"Not really." Rosie stared up at the twilight glimmering through the black silhouetted branches. Little ruffled bird heads were now all snuggled down. "Could it have been an animal, do you think? Crows can be a bit pecky and rough."

Peg frowned. "Rubbish, dear. And there aren't any wolves left in the country anymore."

"No single wizard at supper showed any scratches."

"But who didn't show up?" asked Peg suddenly. "Such a special meal wouldn't normally be missed. So who missed it?"

"Interesting." Rosie bit her lip. "Not counting witches, though I think some might be capable – just counting wizards, I don't think I saw Dandy. Now, I've never liked him. He's fairly strong, a seventy-nine, I think. And it wouldn't surprise me if that sort of man had a dark side."

"Anything's possible. I don't believe Boris came either."

"He often doesn't." Rosie nodded. "And the same with Harry Flash. Only a forty or something, so he likes to keep himself to himself."

The buttercup sprigged grass, attracting dew as the day's warmth ebbed, was now damp, and Peg stood, wishing Rosie a good night. Murder was not something that made her want to stretch out the day.

As Rosie wished her sweet dreams, the bats whirled high in great black sweeps from the thatched roof and the attic beneath, filling the sky with dark clouds before they moved on. Rosie waved goodnight to them too, although it was highly unlikely they would notice her small hand below.

She had rather hoped to see Montague at supper with two nice bright red scratches down his face, but he had come to the table with eager, unblemished smiles. So had Mandrake. Rosie would not have been surprised to discover that Mandrake had a dark side, whereas she had long adored the handsome Montague from a silent distance. He had ignored her, of course, and she doubted if he had even remembered her name. But she had not blamed a wise and powerful wizard for ignoring a pathetic fifty.

That afternoon, however, had changed her mind. He had spoken of her, and then to her, with condescending and patronising insolence and even dislike. Not something to cry about. Something to make her want to punch him in the stomach. Now Rosie even wondered if she had a dark side herself. So she stumbled off to bed and cried herself to sleep.

Having first undressed, Rosie had deposited Oswald on the table beside her and wished him a goodnight. But she had left the retrieved papers, the silver toadstool and silver spoon, and the wrapped handful of her mother's money all hidden within or under the bed.

And as she slept on, dreaming of a miserable future, of dark monsters hiding in the shadows, and of bats flitting down to bite at her neck, she heard nothing of the chatter starting around her bed. Rosie did not, therefore, have any idea that the spoon, toadstool, papers and coins carried on a prolonged conversation in her sleeping absence.

CHAPTER FOURTEEN

"Come on then," Oswald said as the sun rose on the following morning. "Wake up, sleepy head. Time to get up, time to face the questions."

The urgency of his call startled Rosie awake. She regarded the hat pin with surprise. She now always wore Oswald on the neck of her smock, but he rarely spoke to her and generally seemed uninterested in everything going on around them. Now, however, he waited only until she had yawned and stretched, and he then began to relate what had been discussed while she had slept that night.

"Reckon you'd better listen to me," he told her. "We don't know nothing about the new murder. Not our business. But Whistle was my master. He made me. Made the spoon and the cup and the toadstool too. Not to mention all them papers. He liked parchment best, I reckon. Personally, I think paper is better. They're building a paper mill somewhere or another, I think. It'll start getting easier to get hold of soon. Cheaper too. But I reckon 'tis irrelevant. What matters is my master was mighty clever at making magical things."

"Goodness me," mumbled Rosie. "Are you telling me I should buy paper? I still haven't found the cup." She dashed into her clothes with a click of her finger and thumb, brushed her hair with another click and pinned the hatpin on the neckline. "Now I'm supposed to go down and do some work."

"We need to talk first," Oswald insisted. "Have you ever seen a kitten?"

Rosie stared down at her feet, wondering if the hat pin was even more stupid than she had originally supposed. "Lots of kittens," she said patiently. "I love kittens. I always sort of feel I can talk to them. But I only see them in the village. We can't keep cats here because of all the bats and the birds. Most of the cats I see are strays, poor little things, but a lot of the villagers keep them as pets, and the farmers keep them to get rid of mice and rats. But when they have babies, some of the farmers put them in a sack with stones and throw them in a river. I was so upset when I heard that, I cried for three days. Once I rescued one of those sacks and spent all weekend marching around Piddleton finding old ladies who would adopt one of them. I wanted one to keep in my bedchamber, but Mother wouldn't let me. So now," she shook her head, "what on earth are you trying to tell me?"

"Oh, nothing," sighed Oswald. "'Tis clear you ain't ready yet."

"No, not for cats, rats, murder or mayhem," Rosie replied, and hurried down the stairs to collect water, make beds and serve breakfast.

Everyone had now heard of the second horrible murder, and there was no other subject discussed over the breakfast table. They all agreed this had been a shocking act of deliberate cruelty. She was only a maid, after all, and a sad little twelve at that.

"Lowest I ever met," Mandrake said, shaking his head at such a number. "Twelve! Hardly counts as a number at all."

"And the gardener is only a seventeen."

"But he works hard," said Percy. "Slogs away every day, he does. Just needs a bit of seventeen to keep him going."

"Boris isn't much more," whispered Montague, but everyone waved their hands at him and turned away.

"I wasn't much concerned when Whistle went," said Ethelred, quickly changing the subject in case anyone pointed out he was only a thirty-seven. "He was about three hundred years old and the most powerful among us. He could look after himself."

"Obviously not," added Peg.

Vernon Pike, a reasonably healthy sixty-one and therefore just scraping above the important average of sixty, said loudly, "Whistle was an arrogant old codger. Selfish too. Never offered to help anyone."

"Untrue," roared Toby. "He may not have liked you, boob-boy, but he liked me, and we used to play chess together. He always won of course but I didn't mind losing to a ninety-one."

And Rosie, who was busy serving more tiny platters of butter after it had run out, said quickly, "He was lovely to me. And he wasn't rude or condescending just because I'm only a fifty." She glared across at Montague.

But it was the amazing new Edna Edith Enid Ethel Oppolox who quickly answered. "I knew Whistle many years ago," she said as she piled the butter onto another slice of cheese and popped it into her mouth. "A delightful and extremely clever man. We did some work together and were excessively pleased with the result. He usually cheated at chess, because he found just winning too easy. But he never cheated with the magic. Dear Whistle was a pure talent, you know, and a master at creation."

"Still a show-off," muttered Mandrake.

"Perhaps surprisingly," Edna continued, "very high numbers are often embarrassed to speak of it, just as very low numbers are. But I have sincerely enjoyed the company of many low numbers, whereas high numbers – well, I have only known four higher than myself."

Peg was interested. "But not Whistle, since he was only a ninety-one."

"I doubt that," Edna raised a finger. "I imagine his number had grown over the years, but it was pointless wanting a new test, of course. But I count him as one of those higher than myself. There were also sisters I once knew. Delightful both of them, one a ninety-four, and the other poor little thing was just a forty-two. But they were happy together, and I liked both equally. And oh – yes – a man I did not like. He went to the shadows behind the light."

"And the last one?"

"Oh," Edna brushed it aside. "Female, many years ago. I met her only for a moment. But dear Whistle was a great friend before I went to Scotland."

"To live in a cave?" sniggered Vernon.

"It was a very cosy cave." Edna looked down her nose at him. "Or I wouldn't have stayed there."

"But back to Kate," said Peg. "Why would anyone kill a sweet little twelve who helped all of us when we wanted her."

"A bit of a lazy badger," decided Inky. "Not that I'm suggesting that was a reason to bludgeon her to death."

Peg looked up. "How did you know she was bludgeoned?"

"Because you told me half an hour ago," Inky reminded her.

With no one else to do the dishes, Rosie had started cleaning wiping and washing when Edna burst into the kitchen with a sniff, waved one hand so that everything floated around the room cleaning itself in less than a blink and then put itself away. "Come on, my dear," Edna said. "No time to fiddle."

Peg was waiting outside, and they hurried immediately over to the stables. "We must bury the poor child," Edna said. "We have a second attempt at understanding what and why, and then we eliminate the need for that wretched sheriff to visit and interfere."

"The sheriff's assistant isn't too bad," Rosie said.

"Too much of a fool," Peg dismissed him. "After all, my dear, he's a human. Have you ever met an intelligent human? No, well, that's obvious."

Dipper had gone off on his varied trips around the grounds to do the gardening, and Kate's room was unwatched, still containing Kate's lonely body surrounded by the mess of her old life.

With no seeming disgust, Edna bent to pick up the child's corpse and carried it outside and into the sunshine, where she laid it near Whistle's grave. She then hurried back into join Rosie and Peg again. But searching Kate's room brought no surprises and no treasures. When Dipper returned, trudging up to the courtyard with his spade over his shoulder, Peg asked him if he would kindly dig them another grave.

When he heard this was for his neighbour Kate, and marched over to see her remains, he was horrified and exploded into gravelly tears. "It ain't proper," he said, and blew his nose on a piece of rag. "She were a sweet little lass and never did no harm to nobody."

"Murder is rarely proper," Edna told him. "This happened sometime early yesterday, possibly during the night before. Did you hear anything at all?"

"'Fraid not." He looked a little ashamed. "Two nights ago, I were wot you might call a bit tipsy."

"Drunk?"

"Firstly, I were out at the Juggler and Goat, and when I come back home, I just sort of felled into bed. The next day, I felt right poorly and slept again. I doesn't remember much. Reckon I were out like a snuffed candle."

"Shame," Peg sighed. A little upset herself that morning, she had tried to dress herself in calm dark grey, but, as she often did, had got her spell muddled. Now she wore a red and green striped gown with blue ruffles on the neck and cuffs, while her shoes were bright purple slippers with white pom poms. The Rookery, however, was accustomed to Peg's problems and said nothing.

"Did you know?" Rosie asked tentatively, "that Kate stole a few things from time to time?"

"Oh yeh," Dipper replied without shame. "Well, why not? Poor as a primrose, she were. Gotta get a bit together in case she were sent away or got sick or whatnot."

Very pleased with this revelation, Rosie smiled. "And do you know where she hid anything she'd stolen?"

Somewhat reluctant, Dipper eventually nodded. "Well, I reckon you can't call the sheriff on the poor lass now," he said. "So yeh, I reckons I knows. But I'll bury the poor lass first."

Standing in the heat of the sun, Peg, Edna and Rosie watched the sad tumbling of the body into its long narrow hole, and each of them said their own private goodbyes.

"I shall find who did this," Edna promised, "whether that will help you now or not."

Rosie whispered, "Sleep well, Kate."

And Peg, with a fixed scowl, mumbled, "I'm sorry. Very sorry. And so will the vile killer be, once I catch him."

Dipper leaned down and patted the top of his carefully smoothed earth, and snuffled. "'Tis a right shame," he said. "And don't you worry, lass. You doesn't need to steal fer yer old age no more."

There had been the usual faces peering from every window, and Alice had marched out to know what was going on. When told by her own daughter, she pointed out that all orders should be coming from her alone, but since Edna was there, she said no more and marched back indoors.

Back at Kate's room, Dipper opened the shed at the end of the stables and pulled out a small ladder. He tucked this under one arm and burst back into the little room. He leaned it against the wall to one side, which attached to his own room, and climbed the several rungs until his head hit the ceiling. He stretched up one arm and pushed up the ceiling panel behind a thick wooden beam. It seemed to be cracked and wasn't easy to lift, but once Dipper had half crawled into the enclosed shadows beneath the thatch, only his legs visible at the top of the ladder, there was a considerable scuffle heard, and he then reappeared holding a hessian sack. Dipper brought this down and dumped it on the ground, avoiding the rug which remained black with dried blood.

Peg and Edna both insisted Rosie should open the sack, so she turned it upside down and tipped the contents onto the floor of dried earth. She expected scuttling yellow spiders, bad tempered beetles and families of ants, but only one tiny caterpillar made a dash for freedom, while Peg, Edna and Rosie bent down and studied what had been hidden there.

Dipper, uninterested, strode home with a snort of anger at whoever had murdered his neighbour.

Rosie held up a silver bladed knife with a bright blue painted handle. Peg saw and remembered the two embroidered kerchiefs which had once belonged to Emmeline. "All very well stealing from Alice," she said, "but not one of us." She then glanced at Rosie and blushed scarlet. "Sorry, my dear. I didn't mean you. After all, you're nothing like your mother."

Instead, Edna was intrigued by a terra cotta bowl, with a large fish painted on one side, and a lamb on the other. "I do hope your mother doesn't cook real lambs or fish," she said. "This will make a perfect swimming pool for my darling Twizzle."

"No, no real animal gets killed here," Rosie sighed. "And there's no silver cup either. Which is what I wanted. There is a silver platter, but I think it's only plated. There's some money but not much. And there's a few feathers, two pieces of rice paper with nothing written on them, probably Whistle's, and a very pretty silk scarf. Poor Kate, she wouldn't have got enough for a year at most if she'd left The Rookery for any reason."

"So she's left and needs none of it," Edna said with a complete lack of sympathy. "Help yourselves, ladies, or leave it here. Give it to Dipper perhaps. He deserves payment for a very well dug grave."

Pushing everything including the money back into the sack, Rosie dragged it next door, and then the three women walked around to the back of the house where they sat and contemplated the grave.

CHAPTER FIFTEEN

That night Rosie was awakened by a loud tapping on her window. It was still dark, and she guessed it was around midnight or one in the morning. Since she had previously been visited by crows, she assumed the same, although it might be Peg with muddled spells again. Rosie cuddled down under her eiderdown. But the tapping continued, loud and fast. Reluctantly, she peeped from the covers.

Amazed to see her father's face outside the mullions, Rosie grabbed a blanket around her and rushed to open the window. Alfred Scaramouch was barely hanging on to the window ledge, and thankfully climbed into the room, although with difficulty since it was small and he was large.

"I couldn't do the stairs," he whispered, "too noticeable. But I can't fly very well, you see, At least you're only on the first floor."

Fear dripped down her back like icicles, and Rosie shivered. "What's wrong?" Clearly something was terribly wrong, and her father's expression was one of frantic dread.

"My dear," he said, keeping to the whisper, "I believe you may be next."

Rosie stared, face white and mouth open. His meaning could hardly be mistaken. "Me? How do you know?"

Sitting with a bump of relief on the carpeted floor by the bed, Alfred dropped his head in his hands. "I can't tell you everything," he groaned. "But it could be you. I'm not positive, but the risk is too great. You have to leave."

Rosie felt something in her head spinning around and around, and she couldn't think.

"Do you know the killer?"

He shook his head. "But the one obeying orders isn't important," he returned to the whisper.

"So who gives those orders?"

"I can't say." There were large tears rolling down both of his cheeks. "But I care for you too much. You were such a gorgeous baby. So chubby with big brown eyes. No fur."

"Papa, I was a little girl. Not a mouse."

"Yes, yes, my dear, but I adored your little round face and big blue eyes."

Nothing yet made any sense. "That – that's sweet. Thank you. But after all, Papa, I was your daughter."

He looked up. "Oh no," he said, wiping his eyes on his sleeve. "No, I'm not your father, my dearest. No, not at all. But that doesn't matter. I looked after you like a father, and I still love you, my dear. So you have to get out of here and hide somewhere special until all this is over."

There was too much to think about. The swimming buzz gyrating within her head now began to thump and pound. Rosie shut her eyes as the headache grew worse. Lights spangled both inside her closed eyes and outside her head. She tried to summon the spell which would at least clothe her back in her usual smock, and even that failed when she found it was on back to front. So she tried to call Oswald, and then realised he was still pinned to the back of the tunic. Then she silently called to the silver spoon and toadstool, asking them to hide somehow within the wide flax droop of her sleeves. She could not be sure this would work, but was delighted to feel the sudden cold angles of something close to her arms.

With both hands clasped to her head, she scrambled from the bed and bent towards her father.

"Please," she begged, "you have to tell me a little more. Please explain something. Number one, am I adopted? Number two, who wants to kill me? Number three, what have I done?"

Standing, and reaching out to Rosie to help her also stand, Alfred gulped, tottered and croaked, "Adopted? Yes. In a way. Who? I cannot tell you, my sweet. And you haven't done anything. Nothing at all. You're a little angel, and so I told them. But now we have to hurry."

He aimed for the open window, and Rosie followed but squeaked, "Papa, I can't fly either."

"We'll jump," he said, and took her hand.

It had been a day of sunshine, but the night was cold. A wind whistled through the trees, and Rosie remembered Whistle's horrible death and wondered if that was exactly what she now escaped. In a swirl of creamy star spun glitter, the heavens were at peace, but she felt that the world was ending.

They stood together on the narrow window sill, heads bent in order to get through without absolute decapitation. She was so terrified, she could hardly breathe, and Alfred was white-faced with his hair in a knotted cap of tangles.

"One. Two. Three and–" muttered Rosie.

The jump from her window one storey up had jolted her entire body, and her knees felt almost broken, while her headache pounded like a huge drum in her head. Fear made her sick. She doubled over, but Alfred grabbed at her again. "No one saw us," he said hopefully. "Now we run."

"Run where?"

"There's a hollow tree just a little way off."

They ran across the two sad graves, and Rosie noticed her

father was wearing large brown boots with mud on the soles and a bedraggled old cord to lace them up. She heaved again, but kept running.

With neither a cloak nor a blanket to warm her, she was freezing at first, but the rush had done a better job than a cloak, and now she was hot, but could hardly breathe. They passed the tree where Alfred's house had been built and raced beneath where the crows nested, babies now fast asleep nestled beneath their mothers' wings. Kettle Lane meandered off towards the hills beyond, but Alfred did not follow the path and headed towards a great yew tree rising in its strangled twists from an enormous girth into an equally great height. Although at first it looked dead, and the trunk was bent, sufficiently gnarled to be many hundreds of years in age, sprigs of fluttering threads of leaf grew from several of the branches. Within the main trunk and high behind the leafy clusters was a wide uneven hollow, big enough for half of Alfred's overhead cottage.

"There," he said.

"I've got to hide in a dead tree?" Now her heartbeat was louder than her words, and the ramming thunder in her head was louder still. "Must I climb all the way up there? I can't fly. Not unless I hold a hand. And even you couldn't fly that high, Papa."

"I'm not your father," he replied. "Although I wish I was. But don't you know any spells to get you up there?"

She shook her head and wished she hadn't since it was screaming at her. She wanted to be sick. "I don't know proper spells. I'm only a fifty. And I know you're only a twenty, but you're older, and you've learned more than me. And I think I'm going to die. Won't you please explain a little more? Just a little bit? What makes you think I'm next on the list?"

"Because it's almost happened," He said. "Hurry now. You have to go."

"Oh, come on," said a small rough voice behind her. "I'll help."

She wondered who on earth it was, and so did Alfred. Then she realised. "It's Oswald. He's – well, I think Whistle sent him to me." She paused, took a deep breath and asked, "Oswald, can you help me fly up to that hole in the tree?"

"Naturally," said the voice.

Immediately Rosie found herself in the air. She looked down frantically, waved goodbye to Alfred and promptly found herself sitting upright in a large hollow, lined with dry moss, a few old dried leaves and a large sleeping owl cuddled up tight, head buried in its neck feathers as it slept with an occasional humph.

She sank back, didn't want to be sick all over the owl, even though it certainly wasn't Cabbage, and tried desperately to sooth her headache. Finding the space unexpectedly comfortable, Rosie explored. The base was thickly carpeted in leaf and dry moss, creepers and owl feathers. This kept it warm. It was, she decided, like a small wooden cave and not so small at that. She couldn't stand up, but she could lie down if she curled her legs. Indeed, the owl was a very cosy comforter. She simply hoped, as the nest's presumed owner, it would not turf her out once it woke. Already night, and she reminded herself that owls woke and went hunting at night. This one, however, was fast asleep.

With a thousand thoughts in turmoil still spinning in her head, Rosie found sleep impossible, so she twisted her tunic around, mumbled good morning to Oswald with a special thank you for the flight up the tree and pulled out the silver spoon and toadstool. Pressing against the smooth wooden wall at her back, Rosie begged for explanations.

"Am I in danger? Was my father right?"

"He's not your father," sniffed the toadstool.

"Danger, yes," the spoon interrupted. "Imminent? Perhaps. Good idea to hide? Yes indeed."

"So I have to stay here?" It was a terrifying thought.

"Well," said Oswald. "Perhaps not for the rest of your life. Just a few days."

"How do I eat or drink?"

"As a giver of considerable importance," said the spoon with a click of the tongue it didn't actually have, "I shall supply all meals. Being an expert chef, you will eat better here than back in The Rookery."

She was thinking of her mother's magical failures at cooking, when another thought occurred to her. "So," Rosie asked timidly, "is my mother really my mother?"

"Of course not," replied Oswald. "Bad tempered old crow. Nothing like you. And your father – who isn't your father – already informed you about being adopted."

Rosie sank down, confused. "She's just not the type of person I'd expect to adopt a baby. What would she want a baby for? Or was it my father's choice? And who am I? Another witch's baby? Or the child of ordinary humans?"

"Questions, questions, too many questions," objected the toadstool. "I'm going to sleep."

"We need the silver cup," sighed the spoon. "We really don't operate very well unless the three of us come together."

"I never found it," Rosie shook her head. "I searched and searched, but even my mother didn't seem to have it when I looked."

"Not your mother," Oswald reminded her.

But the fear and the confusion, and the thought of living in a tree for weeks were all too much for Rosie, and she promptly burst into tears.

Woken by sobs, the owl fluffed up its wings, looked around and was so startled by what it saw that it jerked wildly and hit its head on the roof of the tree-cave.

"Oh dear, by all the lilac bushes in Wiltshire," it said in a horrified rush, "I've been invaded by aliens."

Rosie stopped crying and apologised. "I mean no harm," she said at once. "But I had to hide. Do you mind? I've got nowhere else to go, but I promise I won't stay too long."

The owl twitched its ears, which were rather long and stuck up from its head in two little dark twists. His feathers, a mottled brown, white and black, were all sitting up on the defensive, and the huge white feathered circles around his staring eyes, seemed a little manic.

"Bother." Then he settled again, deciding there was no instant danger and added gently, "You got anything to eat?"

Rosie turned to the spoon. "Have we?"

"The menu is vast," answered the spoon. "What would you like? Dead rats? Live mice? fish? Tadpoles? Frogs? Bread and cheese? Come on, make a decision."

Eyeing the owl sideways, Rosie muttered, "Fish and dead rats, but not real ones. They just have to taste real. And I'd love some bread and cheese."

The spoon rose and dipped, with all items falling from its scoop. Rosie grabbed the bread and cheese before the owl could get it, while the owl then gobbled everything else. A rat's tail was dangling from his beak when he stared at Rosie with those huge eyes, and said, "I'm pleased to meet you. I presume you're a witch. I'm Dodger."

"I'm Rosie," Rosie said, mouth full. "Don't you go out hunting at night?"

"Not if I can help it," Dodger said. "It's shockingly cold. I see no reason to suffer when it's nice and warm in here. I must say you seem to have an exceptionally useful spoon."

"It would be even more useful," Rosie sighed, "if I could find the missing silver cup."

A thin draught of cold wind had sneaked its way into the yew nest, and both Rosie and Dodger snuggled down, inching closer and closer together for extra warmth. Eventually, as the idea of sleep became more and more attractive, they became positively entangled, and with feathers tickling her nose, Rosie slept with Dodger close beside her.

She had not expected to sleep again, for the confusion and fear felt too great. Yet she sank into an almost immediate doze, for the warmth and protective comfort of the owl brought such peaceful ease, almost like a whispered promise.

It was much later when both Rosie and Dodger woke. Dodger rubbed his head against Rosie's and nibbled at her eyebrow. "Breakfast?" he suggested.

Obediently the spoon also woke, and within moments, both Rosie and the owl were sitting together cheerfully eating scrambled egg on toast with bacon on the side and a cup of orange juice. Dodger turned his beak up at the orange juice, so Rosie drank both cups.

CHAPTER SIXTEEN

That same morning, although a little earlier, Peg and Edna met on the landing outside their two doors and greeted each other warmly.

"I must admit," added Peg in a conspiratorial mumble, "I have now decided you know a good deal more than you've admitted so far, my dear. But you are most certainly intending to help. There's no shadows leaking through."

"Quite right, my dear," smiled Edna. "We are beginning to understand each other very well. I came here for a very special purpose."

Although Peg's hair was a murky grey turning thin white, and she was very small and a little hunched, Edna, once she removed her richly feathered hat of many colours, had bright red hair which hugged her face affectionately. Tall and slim, she appeared much younger than her probable age of more than two hundred, and possibly a lot more. But although the two women were quite different in size and appearance, they were growing inseparable.

Twizzle, hopping from one foot to another, was sitting on Edna's head. Edna did not appear to have noticed, but her bright scarlet hair contrasted neatly with Twizzle's pure white feathers.

"I shall flit down," Peg said, "and see if Rosie is up yet. No doubt she's already making trips to the well. Those buckets must be extremely heavy. Never mind. Soon she'll be able to fetch water by magic."

"And get someone else to do it anyway," Edna nodded.

This, however, was not unknown to Peg now, as she had spent many hours talking with Edna while Twizzle had become bored and sat on the back of the chair muttering, "Hiya, mate, give us a cold beer." So Peg shrugged and flew down the stairs to knock on Rosie's door.

After four knocks with no answer, Peg decided she must already be up working, but just in case, she pushed the door open and peeped inside. She promptly gasped, turned in a flurry and called Edna.

The room was almost entirely upside down. The bed was now attached to the ceiling, and all its covers had fallen off onto the floor with the mattress hanging on by just a few feathers. The little table was stuck to one of the side walls, its legs sticking out, and the small items it had supported were now also on the rug below. One rug was held down since the bed covers had fallen on it, the other rug was flapping about trying desperately to find its proper place. Objects such as candles and Rosie's spare clothes lay in a heap in one corner, and the few papers which Rosie had managed to get from Whistle's collection were no longer where she had hidden them beneath her pillows.

Peg stared, and Edna stood beside her, staring over her shoulder. "Disaster," said Edna in fury. "We have to find the girl as quickly as possible." She clasped both hands to her forehead, attempting to magically decipher Rosie's whereabouts. Peg took the more practical choice, so marched down to the ground floor and started to shout.

"Rosie, Rosie, Rosie. Where are you Rosie?

It was, however, Alice who came from the kitchen. "Yes indeed," she said. "Where is the girl? I have no beds made, no water collected, and no one to help serve breakfast."

Peg certainly didn't offer. "I assume you don't know," she said, "that your daughter's bedchamber has been turned into a madman's chaos. It has been searched and left in a terrible state. And meanwhile Rosie is nowhere to be found."

"No," Alice flung her head back and threw both arms in the air. She shrieked, "Don't tell me that my own beloved daughter has been killed as well?"

Montague and Emmeline had both jumped up from the dining table where they had been sitting waiting for breakfast.

"Who's Rosie?" demanded Montague.

"That dear little girl," moaned Emmeline. "I consider her one of our nicest residents."

"Which is exactly what she is," said Peg. "We have to find her. It could be urgent. It's not as if she might just have gone for a walk or visit the crows or the bats. With her room left in such a state, something is desperately wrong."

"Oh dear," sighed Montague. "Not another nasty wretched murder?"

Edna straightened her shoulders and glared at everyone. "If that girl is found dead like the others," she said, "I shall burn this whole house down."

With equal anger, Alice strode forwards, her hands on her hips. "Don't you threaten my property, madam. Rosie may be my daughter, but I am the householder here, and since I am a personal friend of the local sheriff, I will have you arrested on suspicion of murder."

"I wasn't even here when you had the first one," Edam said, looking suitably autocratic.

Having trudged down the stairs on foot, being another resident incapable of flight, Boris Barnacle looked rather frightened. "Another death? Oh no, I hope not. Not the pretty little maid?"

"Rosie is not a maid," Peg now objected. "She's the owner's daughter. Just sit down and keep out of the way."

Boris nodded. "Woofy woof," he said without emphasis. "I always do as I'm told. Plumpetty Plod."

"Is the man mad?" whispered Edna.

"Who cares," Peg said loudly. "I'm off to find Rosie."

Alice did not seem too worried. "The girl's useless at the best of times. I expect she's up playing with Cabbage, or she's gone for a walk to the village."

"Not this early," Edna said, and she and Peg hurried from the kitchen out the back where the two sad graves lay in the rising sunshine. The grass was quickly growing over the two slight mounds, and Whistle's little hillock already sprouted a daisy.

On one side of The Rookery was the well, and on the other side a row of three privies. The front gazed out onto Kettle Lane. At first, Peg ran one way and almost fell into the well, whereas Edna ran the other way but turned back because of the smell.

Meanwhile, discussing the advantages of magic, Rosie and Dodger were becoming the best of friends. Dodger was particularly interested to hear all about Cabbage. "And she's a she?" he asked. "I'm a he. Hes and shes usually get along. I'd like to meet your Cabbage."

Rosie thought Cabbage might very well enjoy meeting Dodger too, but said, "I'm afraid I can't leave this nice cosy tree until someone tells me it's safe. But I could explain how to get to her, and then you could just mention that I sent you."

Dodger's smile was quite impossible to distinguish from his normal wide-eyed expression, but Rosie assumed he was smiling. "Brilliant idea," he said. "I shall go this evening. Now, explain the route."

"With someone flying easily like you," Rosie explained, "I think you'd only take a moment. Cabbage lives in the thatched roof of the main house called The Rookery, right in the middle of the actual rookery on Kettle Lane." Rosie pointed in the right direction. "I'm sure she'll be pleased. Cabbage is awfully sweet."

"And so am I," said Dodger. "So we're bound to get on well." He thought of something and turned his head in a feather less than a full circle, and added, "But what sort of owl is she?"

"Same as you. A long-eared owl. Big and lustrous with beautiful eyes. Yes, just like you."

"And," Dodger continued, "I should be delighted to help all those who help me. So where is this silver cup you keep mentioning. I gather it's important?"

"Well, yes." Rosie was curled on the moss, hugging her knees. The silver spoon and toadstool appeared to be asleep, but Oswald remained very much awake. "The trouble is, I have no idea where it is. I searched over and over. But my silver spoon and the silver toadstool can do wonderful magic, if only they have the silver cup with them. Then it has to rain – not sure why – and with all three of them together, they can make wonderful things happen. And now that I'm in danger, I need wonderful things even more urgently."

The gruff little voice from Oswald muttered, "Not rain, silly-billy-Rosie. Water. Any kind of water. But rain would be good. After all, this is England, isn't it?"

Ignoring this interruption and with a wiff and a toowit, Dodger settled down to think. "Where would you guess," he asked eventually, "in or out?"

"I assume you mean the house, but it doesn't matter, because it could be either."

"A large cup?" he said. "or a tiddly one?"

Immediately Rosie asked Oswald. The hat pin was more helpful than usual. "It is quite large," Oswald said, "but no more than a breakfast cup of ale. All nice shiny silver, and inside on the bottom is a nice big 'W' standing for Whistle. Heavy too, being solid."

"I think it's probably in the kitchen," Rosie sighed. "I've searched in so many places, and I can't see my mother allowing anyone else to look after it. She'd want it under her thumb. I know she must have it, unless Whistle himself hid it before he was killed."

"Silly idea," sniffed Oswald. "Whistle needed it every day. No point hiding it away."

"Kate didn't have it," Rosie said. "And it isn't in my mother's bedroom, unless it was in the last chest under the bed which I couldn't open. Very possible I suppose. So either there or in the kitchen."

"Not a problem," Dodger lay his head on Rosie's shoulder. "I shall discover this elusive cup. I shall befriend the glorious Cabbage. And I shall keep you safe."

Rosie gave him a hug. She realised he was quite thin inside all those fluffy layers of feathers and down, and she asked Oswald to summon up some more pretend dead rats.

As the day grew warmer, Rosie started to doze. At once Dodger put his left wing over her, and she snuggled into the shadow. Both slept as the sun angled within the little wooden hollow, and soon everything was a shimmer of warmth.

Neither Edna nor Peg stopped to eat, drink or chat. They did not even fly, for such a fast way of travelling made it difficult to notice anything on the way. So the two women marched the stairs up and down in every direction. They questioned the bats, and they insisted on entering every single resident's room. But although they had a good excuse, they were not always welcome.

Pixie was delighted to let them in. "I made this myself," she pointed to the bed, four posts and a huge yellow velvet tester hanging above it. "Took me ages. I'm a seventy-six, so hardly useless, but the tester just never looked right. So I was determined to make it by hand. I'm exceedingly proud of the result. And my patchwork eiderdown, isn't this beautiful?"

Gorgeous, on the other hand, was exceedingly shy and tried to explain why her room was practically empty. As a timid nineteen, she could hardly produce anything at all.

"Ask me," said Peg. "I should be only too delighted to help."

They moved on to the large Butterfield room, with a window so wide they could see half the garden. From there to Lemony who had transformed her room into a bright yellow mock bee's nest for no obvious reason, but the smell of fresh honey was delightful.

"Honey?" She held out a jar. Both Peg and Edna were pleased to accept.

Most of the men's rooms were considerably less tidy, although Mandrake's quarters were a model of beautifully painted gloss. On the other hand, Ethelred, Montague, Boris and Percy were grubby, untidy and unattractive. Boris had a black ceiling and a few drips of black paint while Montague had all his precious clothes hanging from the ceiling in long rows. Percy was a little ashamed of his mess, but Ethelred was impatient, told them to hurry and get out since he was busy.

Having searched the entire house for Rosie, Peg and Edna proceeded to the stables. Dipper was out, but they looked in his room anyway. It was full of flowers growing in pots, under the bed, on two long shelves and on the window sill. Peg smelled the gush of wonderful perfumes and almost sat down there to breathe in some more. Edna, however, pulled her on.

They spent some time discussing the problem with the crows, but each one protested that they knew nothing and Rosie was certainly not hiding amongst them.

Finally, and with considerable hope, both Edna and Peg flew up to Alfred's treehouse and knocked politely on the door. There was no answer, so Peg called softly, "Rosie, my dear. Are you there?"

No one answered, and so Edna opened the door with a finger flick, and the two women stepped inside.

The chaos within was similar to everything they had seen in Rosie's room, and both Peg and Edna stepped back in alarm. The snug salon on the ground floor and the cosy attic bedchamber both lay in ruins. Some furniture appeared stuck to the ceiling or walls, as Rosie's had been, and smaller items were scattered everywhere across the floor. But Alfred Scaramouch, neither living nor dead, was present amongst the mess.

He had clearly received some warning and had escaped before the intruder arrived. And there was, most certainly, no sign of Rosie.

A small brown rabbit was hiding beneath the upturned jug of water. Peg help it out. "Well, well," she said, smiling, "I'm exceedingly sorry for whatever you've suffered and whatever you've seen. But I'm exceptionally pleased to find I have a witness. Now, tell me everything that happened."

"Alfie went out in the middle of the night," quavered the rabbit. "And he never come back again. I was waiting in the hope of a little breakfast. But then this fellow comes marching in. Strong, he was, and kept puffing sparks and flames, real terrifying so I hid under the table, but then the jug fell on top and I couldn't get out. This fellow, he wore big brown boots, all scruffy like. In a big hat and a big cloak, so I couldn't see no more. But he wrecked the joint, like you can see. Got more and more angry. Clearly he couldn't find what he were looking for. Was ages here, but then he done stomped off. This place used to be so nice and calm and safe."

"Well, not anymore," said Edna between her teeth.

.

CHAPTER SEVENTEEN

Extremely disappointed and even more worried, Peg and Edna sat on the long low bench at the back of the grounds and watched the daisies growing on Whistle and Kate's graves.

At some distance, a long walk or a short flight, Rosie was bored stiff. Comfortable as the nest was, there was nothing for her to do except talk to a hat pin, a spoon, a toadstool and an owl. None of them had anything interesting or pertinent to say. Dodger spent most of the day asleep, and although Oswald was very helpful in summoning various feasts, he kept telling her it was too early to explain anything in detail.

"Just explain roughly then."

"Pointless," Oswald told her.

The spoon and the toadstool persisted in saying they had been made as a threesome, and without the silver cup, they could not operate properly.

"I give," said the spoon. "He," pointing to the toadstool, "takes. And then the cup fills with the answer."

"Bother," muttered Rosie with a yawn. "You'd think two out of three would be useful at something. It's most frustrating. And all

I've done all day long is peep outside, shift my position a hundred times and eat."

"And talk endlessly to yourself," mumbled the toadstool.

After a supper of dead rats and roast pork with spinach in cream and sultanas, Dodger became excited and hopped happily from one foot to another while ruffling his feathers and combing out his wings. Clearly wishing to look his best, the owl admitted he was going to visit Cabbage, hopefully before she went out hunting for herself.

"I have plans," he said. "Just you wait and see. We owls are very wise, you know."

She didn't want him to go. It had been boring enough while he slept, but now to spend several hours entirely alone seemed like prison. From misery, she quickly moved on to greater despair, wondering how on earth she would manage to last several days like this. The thought of finding the silver cup was a wonderful hope, but she felt it most unlikely. But she smiled and waved Dodger goodbye and good luck. "Have fun," she told him. "And don't kill too many sweet little animals."

With the contempt it deserved, Dodger ignored this last remark and flew off into the night. The stars had not yet found the path through the clouds, and the sky remained misty and without drama. Rosie, with no other option, moved to the back of the nest, curled up again, shut her eyes and wondered if some nasty old witch or wizard had cursed her.

Curses weren't easy, even for the shadow kings, but there had been stories of shocking curses laid on both the guilty and the innocent in the past. Hard things to lift as well, except by a good witch or wizard of somewhere in the eighties or nineties. Edna would be a valuable witch to have around, Rosie decided, and Peg was not too far behind. Yet Whistle, a wonderful ninety-one or more, had been the first to die.

Still thinking of such matters, Rosie eventually wound her head into boring loops and gradually fell asleep. She was dreaming of comfy mattresses, nice clean tables and warm blankets when she woke suddenly.

Two owls, huge-eyed were gazing down at her from the opening. Behind them was a vast shining silver moon, and in Dodger's beak was a shining silver cup. Rosie sat up in such a hurry, she bumped her head and twisted her ankle but could hear Oswald complaining from beneath her chin.

"You found it? Miracle upon miracles. Oh, you wonderful marvellous beautiful birds. Thank you, a million times over."

Dodger and Cabbage seemed to think Rosie had gone a little mad, and both stared down at her.

"Your directions were excellent," Dodger informed her. "I made the acquaintance of this admirable lady Cabbage, and explained the situation. She quite understood since she had been a friend of your early wizard-loss and told me about the recent chaos. She explained it had been unwise to enter the house for days, and therefore she was content to accept my company. I then recounted your need for a silver cup, which might be in a chest under the bed of your estimable parent, the official owner of the establishment. We were able to enter her room through the window, and since she was still in the kitchen, we were quick to pull out the chests from below the bed. With both beaks together, we had little trouble except on the second, which was too heavy. But, in any case you declared that the probable chest was at the end, and we were quick to open it."

"Really? I couldn't find the spell. What did you say?"

"Oh, the usual rubbish," Dodger said. "Clearly this woman is no great spell-maker. Just that twaddle stuff. *'Tie me up tight and hide me from sight, Open at your leisure, there's nothing to measure. Just say please and I'll open with ease.'*"

Rosie actually felt a little annoyed with herself for not having remembered this age-old spell, but she leaned forward eagerly and took the cup from Dodger's beak. It was surprisingly heavy. Leaning back down again, she rubbed her hands carefully across it, thrilled to have it at last. It seemed doubly precious. Finally, she set it down between the spoon and the toadstool, and was delighted all over again when they all seemed to wake and began to dance together, bobbing and bouncing up and down, whirling around and generally welcomed the newcomer with silent glee.

Leaving her to her own business, which both owls thought most peculiar, Dodger and Cabbage flew up into one of the higher branches and chattered together. It appeared to be love at first sight.

Rosie meanwhile took a very deep breath, "Have you a name?" she asked the cup, trying not to start her own questions too abruptly.

The following silence echoed, but eventually the cup began its own discussion. "I have no name," it announced. "A pointless accessory. You are girl. I am cup. This is spoon, and that is toadstool. Outside are female owl and male owl. What more do you need? It is true you all claim names, since you value your individual identity, but I have no wish for such childish nonsense."

Hurrying past all this, Rosie asked, "Do you know of the recent terrible problems at The Rookery? You must surely know your wonderful maker Whistle was brutally killed by someone we haven't yet discovered." She leaned very close, as if frightened the essential answer might escape her. "Do you know who killed him?"

"Yes," said the cup.

A trifle disappointed at receiving just that one word, Rosie asked, "Who?"

"Man," said the cup with the same refusal to use names. "Not too tall. Not too fat. Not too slim. Not too intelligent. A red doublet beneath a red and gold coat over blue knitted hose. Not a pretty sight. Brown boots, heavy and unclean. Dark shadows within."

"His hair?" she asked, already worried.

"Short, off the ears, nondescript. Not pale. Not dark."

"And how did his boots fasten?"

"Old cords. Pale in colour but grubby."

The cup's answers were clear and concise, but he had described her father, and Rosie had to gulp and bite her lip to stop the tears. She sank back and regarded all three of the silver items which evidently Whistle had made himself and had regarded as important. Perhaps essential. "I have to explain something," she said, trying to hold back the sniffs. "I was told I was in danger and had to come and hide. Is that true?"

"Which?" said the cup.

Now she wanted to hit it. "I know it's true I was told this," she said patiently. "But is it true I was in danger?"

Here, the spoon interrupted. "I hate to interrupt," it said, unmoving, "but talking to cup alone is not in your best interests. As the giver, I should give a little good advice. We need water first. A little lubrification will bring cup to his senses and he will be far more explanatory."

"But," Rosie said, feeling even more dismal, "it isn't raining."

"No, no," said the toadstool with a small snort. "Just water."

"Clean water," the cup insisted. "Streams around, no doubt. Rain water collected in pots. As you wish. Then fill the spoon and drink it. Fill the toadstool through its etched holes and drink it. Then fill me with nice sparkly water and finally drink it. Have a belch or whatever you wiccan folk liked to do after gulping water, and then you can ask whatever comes into your small head. Depending on the question, toadstool will take, spoon will give, and I shall collect and explain the answer."

Then Dodger poked his head back in to see what was happening. "Sun up in a few moments," he pointed out. "Dear Cabbage and I will now return to the thatched home you call The Rookery, and I shall stay with my dear Cabbage for the day's sleep. I'm very fond of thatch and even more fond of Cabbage. You may stay here in peace. Do you wish me to carry a message to anyone at your home?"

"What a wonderful idea," she told him, brightening at once. "Yes, please. Two witches, one short, one tall. Peg and Edna. And tell them where I am. But please, oh please, don't tell anyone else. Don't even tell Peg or Edna if other people are listening. If the message can't be utterly private, then I'd prefer you to say nothing at all."

He nodded with a bristle of feathers. "I shall indeed. And, dear friend, do pop up to the nest in the thatch one day. Darling Cabbage and I would love to meet you again."

The faint line of promised sunshine had painted the horizon. The few stars blinked out. The great round moon, an important symbol to the wiccan folk, was westing behind the hills. The barely visible crack between sky and land widened as the sun attempted to slide further up.

Rosie watched as the two owls, great wings spread wide but utterly silent, flew out into the streaks of pink and lilac. Then as the owls disappeared into the distance, the pink turned scarlet and the lilac turned golden. A vast parade of colours lit the eastern sky, and Rosie leaned back. She knew without words that everything was going to be alright.

For a moment she closed her eyes, then opened them again and stared down at the three silver objects on the moss beside her. "Do you know," she asked softly, "where there's a stream or a pond? A lake? A river? I don't know any around here."

With a small rattle, the toadstool shook its spots. "No idea, lady," it said. "You want answers, you'd best go and look."

Disappointed, she realised that at risk of being seen and spoiling everything, she had to go back in the direction of The Rookery and visit the well. But then she realised she had nothing in which to carry the water once she'd brought it up. She could, perhaps, take all three objects with her and fill them with water while actually beside the well, but this would be an even greater risk. She could not only be caught by the killer himself, but would lose her three precious silver items.

There was no answer in her mind, and she stared around, could not think of a thing, wondered if she could make something out of old wood, doubted it and, feeling stupid and helpless, began to cry.

The beauty of the sunrise after the sight of the full moon had brought her a shiver of magical happiness. Now she felt the absolute opposite, for she knew herself to be ridiculously powerless, could not use the silver objects she had wanted so much, even though she now had them. What was more, the affectionate hugs from her father blurred back into her mind.

Yet he was not her father at all. What was more, he might well be the murderer.

A faint call interrupted her depression. "My dear Rosie, are you there?"

"Can you see us, dear?"

She knew both voices and rushed to the opening, leaning out with a huge smile down at the two little faces staring up from so far below. One short woman with a tiny white cap and a few straggles of white hair beneath. The other's face had disappeared beneath a richly feathered hat.

"I'm coming," Rosie called. "Oh, thank you and bless you, and you're both just wonderful. I'm coming."

CHAPTER EIGHTEEN

"And we still don't know who, why or even a proper what."

"We shall sit in a circle, my dear, here in my room, just where dear Whistle sat to create his wonderful spells and devices. What better place?" Edna had set up three chairs around her small table, and on the table sat the silver cup, the toadstool and the spoon. Between them was a large earthenware jug full of cool clean water.

Rosie, sitting on the middle chair, had moved Oswald to a more visible position, still pinned to her tunic but now on the loose belted waist. There were three huge smiles around the table, and only Oswald was complaining. "No drink for me, I suppose?"

The sunshine spun its own web through the window mullions, and the light was a glitter of promise.

"Right," said Peg, through her grin. "Let's begin."

"You first, dear," Edna told Rosie.

Rosie shook her head, a little embarrassed. She had been flown from the tree nest all the way to her father's tree house and had been shocked at the ruin there. It gave her comfort now believing her father could surely not be the killer, although that was not yet positive. Yet why? Nothing made the slightest sense to her.

Rosie had then been flown directly in through Edna's window, and was now sitting comfortably in Whistle's old room. Yet after a day and two nights in the owl nest, she was aching all over and kept sneezing with feathery scraps of down up her nose. The headache had eased, but every other ache was vibrant and seemingly had no intention of leaving. Rosie's mind was certainly not functioning as clearly as she would have liked. Although the misery of self-pity had flown with her own flight, she still remained horribly conscious of being so weak in the presence of others so considerably stronger.

"You first, Peg," Rosie said. "I'm not really feeling clever this morning."

"I am not surprised," Peg answered her. "But I do feel we should grab this glorious opportunity as quickly as possible, in case something else goes wrong. And I couldn't possibly do this without you beside me, dear."

"And," Edna looked up, her hand on the water jug, "I do think it should be you, Rosie, my dear, who should do this little water trick."

Rosie sighed but took the jug and carefully poured some water through the holes in the toadstool. She spilled half the water, but no one seemed to care. Then she lifted the toadstool to her mouth and drank back the water she had just poured in. She then copied the same procedure with the spoon, and this time spilled even more. But she drank and felt remarkably refreshed. "Last one," she said, and poured water into the cup. After all she had spilled, there was only just enough. But the cup was brimming as she picked it up between her palms and drained it.

The tiredness disappeared. Then, as she sat forward, one by one, every single ache in her body faded away. Gradually her entire body felt joyously young. She wanted to dance. She almost wanted to sing.

Edna was watching her with considerable interest. "You want to ask the questions after all, don't you, my dear? Then, please, go ahead."

She didn't know how brightly her eyes were shining, but Rosie smiled at the three silver items on the table, rubbed a small finger over Oswald and said quite loudly, "Who is my real father?"

"I take away Alfred Scaramouch," said the toadstool.

"And I give the proper name," said the spoon,

The cup tipped up and then settled. It spoke even more loudly and said, "Whistle Hobb."

Rosie's delight and energy dropped. "That's impossible," she whispered. Peg and Rosie were staring, but Rosie noticed Edna was not.

"We cannot ever be wrong," the cup pointed out. "But it is your choice whether to believe it or not."

"Then," Rosie said, this time after a great exhale, "who is my mother? I cannot believe that Mamma was ever Whistle's wife."

"I take away Alice Scaramouch," said the toadstool.

"And I have nothing to give," said the spoon.

So the cup said, "You do not have one."

After a very short and shocked silence, Peg and Rosie both spoke together. "Impossible."

Peg hurried on. "We are witches, and Whistle was a great wizard, but we must all still have a mother. Without a mother, no baby can be born."

Rosie was shaking her head in bewilderment. "I'm glad it's not Alice. So very, very glad. But all this is so hard to take in. And I have to have a mother. Emmeline is always so sweet to me," she suggested. "It has to be someone, even if she's not living at The Rookery." She turned to Peg. "I wish it was you, Peg. I'd be so proud to call you my mother."

But the cup simply repeated its previous statement. "You do not have a mother."

After the initial excitement, the following disappointment – and now this, Rosie wasn't sure she could believe anything else the cup told her. She leaned back in the chair, closed her eyes and asked, "Who killed Whistle and Kate?" She was sure if the cup told her it was her father, who wasn't her father, she would throw the cup through the window and go to bed in tears.

But after the usual taking and giving, the cup said, "Boris Barnacle."

And once again everyone stared at everyone. Even Edna no longer seemed complacent.

"He's close to the last person I'd have expected," Peg frowned. "A very weak magical power, and a funny little man who usually speaks rubbish, either bored or just too stupid."

Sighing, Edna reached out, smoothing her fingers around the top of the cup. "But we cannot simply dismiss everything we're being told. These beautiful objects are Whistle's own creations. How can we possibly believe we know better than this, when we actually have no idea?"

"I thought," Rosie said, turning to Edna, "that perhaps you did know something. When the cup said my father was Whistle, which is just preposterous, you didn't even look surprised."

"It's the one thing about you I do know," Edna said, eyes suddenly large. "I have no idea who this Boris person might be. And I find it hard to imagine a child being born without a mother. However, my dear, I came here to do justice to Whistle, who was once my greatest friend in all the world, and I am inclined to trust his magical inventions."

"I think I want to go to bed," said Rosie.

"Then I think," concluded Edna, "you should sleep in my room, dear. Indeed, I insist. I think you are still in danger. Sleep here, and I shall put spells on both the door and the window. You will not be disturbed."

"I'll be disturbed anyway," she mumbled. "I feel like a mouse in a trap. And none of this is supposed to be about me. I just wanted to find who killed Whistle, and then Kate."

"Perhaps Boris after all?"

"Anything is possible," frowned Edna. "But apart from putting a spell on the door and the window, I feel I should put a spell on you, my dear. You must sleep long and deep." And she raised both hands. "Climb into bed, dear."

With a long habit of obedience, Rosie clambered onto the vast soft mattress, snuggled down into the amazing comfort and closed her eyes. Within three seconds, she was asleep.

It was much later when she started to dream. Whistle was sitting on a cloud.

"Why don't you want me for a father, child? Most unappreciative."

"Number one, I hardly know you, and you hardly know me. Number two, you're a ninety-three or something and I'm a fifty—"

"Let me interrupt you here and now," Whistle said, crossing his shirt striped legs, "you are not a fifty. You might be a two hundred and forty-six for all you know."

"That doesn't exist."

"Ah," exclaimed the vision. "So already you know better, eh? Says she's a lowly fifty, but then insists she knows better than me."

"Come on then, wise wizard. What is this murder and mystery all about, and what has it got to do with me anyway?" The dream-state Rosie was also sitting on a cloud, pink, which was remarkably soft and both warm and dry. "I know you aren't my father, but if Alice isn't my mother, I'd be quite pleased. It would be hard to get used to, but I really don't like her."

"No," nodded the apparition. "I made a bad choice."

"To be the mother of *your* child?"

"Not really. Much more complicated," Whistle said. "Go and read some of my papers."

"They've been stolen, torn up, burned and lost," said Rosie with slight confusion.

"So get the damned things back," said Whistle with a bit of a shout. "You've got my toadstool, spoon and cup, for heaven's sake. And you have dear Oswald. I made a special point of whizzing you off a couple of weeks ago, not so easy when you're dead, you know, just to make sure you got Oswald, and now you've hardly made any use of him at all."

Even the dreaming Rosie had to stop and think about this. Yes, indeed, she had been very suddenly spun into a nowhere land and then returned safely with the addition of one remarkable hat pin, pure ruby and quite chatty.

So she nodded "I'll talk to Oswald again, but he doesn't know who killed you. Surely you know yourself?"

"Actually," replied the floating wizard, "I didn't at first, since he crept up on me from behind. I didn't feel a thing. Anyway, he's not important."

And Rosie woke to the rich smell of pea, leek and cream soup with plenty of buttered chunks of bread.

With delight, Rosie sat, accepted the bowl and spoon, not the huge silver one, but an average sized tin one with a bit of a bump in the middle, and said between mouthfuls, "I dreamed of Whistle."

Peg sat on the edge of the bed while Edna settled herself on a large cushioned chair. "It's hard to judge dreams," said Peg. "But I do agree that Whistle is at the bottom of all this. So I am going to try and bring back all his papers. Some are bound to bring solutions and answers. I think we might learn a lot." She stood, and Rosie saw she was carrying another large jug of water. Smiling back at Rosie, Peg asked, "You or me, dear? I still believe it should be you."

Although the silver trio's answers had not convinced her in the slightest, Rosie remembered the glorious refreshment the second hand water had brought. She longed to experience that again, so she cheerfully agreed, hopped out of Edna's bed and went to sit at the table once more. This time, with a far steadier hand and more confidence, she poured the water from the jug into the toadstool and then drank. As it had claimed, it took away. Rosie immediately realised it had taken away her remaining aches, her fuzzy thoughts and her worried confusion. So she filled the spoon from the jug and drank carefully. The spoon gave, and so now she was given clear thoughts and a sense of blissful rejuvenation. Finally, the cup. She filled it right up to the brim. Not a drop spilled as she drank.

Then Rosie leaned back with an enormous smile of satisfaction. She felt wonderful and was sure she could achieve whatever she wished. Life was suddenly glorious.

"Ask for every single one of Whistle's papers, books and parchments to be returned," Peg murmured. "Brought back from whoever has taken them, but also reproduced if any were destroyed."

As Rosie spoke the words, a flap of breeze started to whirl and swirl, suddenly switching to flocks of white mist. Then the mist cleared, edges becoming sharp and clear. White merged with traces of black, then the black snatched up the white, still zooming into unravelling circles. White controlled black once more, the papers were visible as they flew, then a little slower, and finally fluttered into a soft surrender. Now the papers lay still, covering the table, the bed, the three skirted laps and most of the floor.

"Claws, beaks and wings," Peg exclaimed. "There are more than I'd realised. It will take a year to read them all." Three scrolls of parchment had balanced on her head, and one was unrolling with eager anticipation.

"Me first," it squeaked.

"I do wish you weren't all so eager," Rosie sighed, trying to stop one small piece of papyrus from climbing inside the neck of her tunic.

Edna wasn't listening. She had turned back to Rosie. "Tell the papers they must arrange themselves," she said. "Any of them related to the same subject must club together. Letters to him from other people in a separate pile. Organisation in general, and the most recently written papers on top."

Rosie smiled. "Yes, all of that," she said without bothering to repeat anything, and at once the papers began to flutter again. "Most obliging of you," she added.

"Exhausting," a tome looking like a beautiful prayer book mumbled, flapping open and showing it was actually a book of spells.

"I'm unique," said a folded paper. "I won't fit with anything else." But within a few moments, the papers sat in four neat piles, the first being gigantic, and about to topple over.

Peg grabbed this, and Edna said, "This is an excellent beginning. "I shall leave you in peace, my dear, since you've been looking forward to reading all Whistle's thoughts and experiments. There should be a few good new spells mixed up in there. And, of course, some clues. That's what we want most of all. And you, my dear, are the expert in runes and translations, as long as you remember not to stand on your head." She stood, nodding towards Rosie. "Meanwhile, I think I shall go for a walk with Rosie. A very open and obvious walk, so everyone can see her. And I shall be watching each passing face and how they look at her."

"Must I?"

"I think it's important, my dear. With me, I promise you will be entirely safe, since I'm on my guard, and a ninety-three being particularly watchful really cannot be beaten. I need to see the reactions. Some more than others, of course, but everyone is relevant."

"Especially Boris."

"Boris, Alice, and a few others," smiled Edna without explaining.

CHAPTER NINETEEN

B oris nodded and said, "Hoppity hop, flopperty flip."
Alice glared. "How dare you run off, stupid girl," she said, glaring, eyebrows in a rigid line of distaste. "No buckets of water when I need them, no beds made, no one to serve meals, no one to help at all."

With her new confidence exaggerated by the water from the silver trio, Rosie waved and put her nose in the air. "Poor Kate was the maid, and it didn't exactly make her life a happy one. Go and employ someone else. You can afford it."

Alice's eyes narrowed, cold and furious. "How do you know what I have or don't have?"

"You'd be surprised," Rosie laughed at the eyebrows. "By the way, you look like a troubled caterpillar. You should send one of the men for those horrible heavy buckets and make your own bed."

Rosie trotted off before Alice could stagger back from the shock. Edna led her around to the meeting hall, past the stables, beneath the crows' rookery and back into every shadowed corner, corridor and dining room. A few people waved. Emmeline said she was glad to see her again and offered a lump of chocolate, which

Rosie later shared with Edna, and they finally ended up in Rosie's own bedchamber.

Standing aghast in the open doorway, Rosie stared at the mess which had once been her own tidy little shelter, where she could dream alone and escape her mother. Now she saw her best tunic torn on the floor, the eiderdown she had made herself screwed in a heap and her nice polished table stuck fast to the wall. The bed stared back at her. The four legs seemed glued to the ceiling, and all the covers had tumbled. Rosie felt like crying again.

She was jolted from her complacency. "That's – horrible," she said, trying to stop her knees shaking. "Talk about making the beds. I can't even reach mine. It's upside down on the ceiling."

"So why?" demanded Edna.

"I own nothing valuable. Nothing even interesting." And then she realised. "My father – that's Alfred – he came in the middle of the night, really scared, poor man. He told me to run, because I was in terrible danger. *Next on the list,* he said. So I did, and I hid where he told me and where you found me. But I took the silver things with me. I bet that was what someone was looking for." Pausing again, she thought of Kate. "Kate took the toadstool and the spoon when she cleaned up Whistle's room. She stole them, but when I asked her about things, she offered them both if I paid, which I did."

"And the cup?"

"Dodger the owl brought it to me while I was in his nest. Sounds a bit odd, doesn't it? He found it in my mother's chest of secrets hidden under her bed. But," she added, "I should have asked him what else he saw in that chest. I never thought of it. I was just desperate."

"I'm not sure it matters," Edna said. "We'll see. If we decide it matters one day, we can walk back to the hollow yew tree and ask him."

"Easier than that," Rosie said. "He's living upstairs with Cabbage now. Romance."

"Humph. Very sweet, I'm sure," said Edna with evident sarcasm.

"Now let us get back to Peg and the papers. I imagine she's read quite a few by now."

She had. Peg was engrossed, her nose in the various papers which surrounded her, but she stopped, looking up as Rosie and Edna entered.

"I have an important mission," Peg said, leaning back in the chair and crossing her arms. Being rather short, her feet did not reach the rug, and were dangling half way. Yet her expression was in no manner child-like. "You and I, Edna, are going to do something you know about, but I've never done before."

Edna nodded, "I know what you're thinking of, my dear. An excellent idea." I shall guide you."

"Whistle's papers are hard to follow," Peg continued. "Some are completely indecipherable. And sadly, I assume the most urgent and important ones are those he put in such difficult code. But one thing is clear as rat droppings. This whole business is dreadfully important and involves Whistle, Alice and Rosie."

"Me again?" Rosie sank onto another of the chairs. "And my wretched mother?"

Edna moved away the papers, piling them on the bed with Peg's help. She then moved the silver objects and took them into the second room. Lastly, she held out her hand to Rosie. "May I have that dear little hat pin you chat to?" she asked. "I have a good reason, as I'm sure you can guess, and you shall have it back very soon."

With a sigh, Rosie unpinned Oswald and handed him over. Oswald shouted, "What a cheek, old lady. I go where I want." But Edna took no notice and bundled him off into the other room.

They sat as they had before, in a circle around the small table, but this time the table was bare without jugs of water or anything else.

"Right. I shall start," said Edna softly. "Close your eyes, my dear, then listen carefully to everything you hear. No looking. Just hearing."

Rosie knew her neck and shoulders were rigid, and tried to breathe deeply without worry or strain.

"Nothing matters, dear," Edna continued. "You will not even understand some of what I will say. But I shall ask twenty-four questions, and you will answer whatever comes into your head. There are no wrong answers. Actually, there are no right ones either. Now," and she clicked her fingers. Immediately Rosie realised she had relaxed so completely that she almost believed she was sinking through the chair and through the floor.

"Umm," she said, although she'd had no intention of speaking, "I am entirely ready."

"Good," Edna smiled. "So, first question. You like numbered lists. So number one. Where are your primary feathers?"

It didn't bother her, but Rosie felt this to be a rather stupid question. "I don't have wings," she said. "And my only feathers are up my nose from Dodger's nest. My actual wings are my powers. But if you want a more relevant answer, then waddle and snot."

"Excellent," said Edna to Rosie's great surprise. "An excellent answer. Now, number two. What would you do if someone tried to hit you?"

"Stop him," said Rosie with a faint sniff.

"Good, good," Edna said, scribbling with her finger in a sort of notebook enclosed in leaves.

Peg was busy nodding. "Now tell me how old you are, dear."

"Twenty-four and a few months and several days, plus no end of hours and so on. But," she concluded, "it's of no importance whatsoever. Not only has my mother forgotten my birthday, but now I think I have as well. Besides, age is utterly useless for understanding anything. Idiots can be twenty-four too. They can be nasty, and they can be nice, and that's far more interesting than how old they are. Most of the folk in The Rookery are way over two hundred, and every one of them is entirely different from everyone else. Power makes a difference, but years do not. Individuality is what makes a character, not age."

She knew it was her voice and could hear it, but Rosie was sure she hadn't said any of it. She tried to say so but nothing came out.

Once again, Peg took the turn. "Now then, where is Whistle?"

The voice inside Rosie's head clicked again. "He's inside Oswald, but he's fast asleep. When I decide to wake him, he'll pop back in. Then I'll have Whistle when he's awake, and when he falls back asleep, I'll have Oswald. I shall know how to wake Whistle when it becomes important. Not yet."

"Choose a number. Any number," said Edna suddenly.

"Ninety-eight," Rosie said off the top of her head.

"Really?" Edna was interested. "Right, who are your parents?"

"Alice and Alfred Scaramouch are my adopted parents," Rosie replied, surprising herself. "Whistle chose them when he needed a mother and father for me. They were a poor choice, especially Alice, but then Whistle knew very little about parents himself having forgotten his own years back. My real parents are difficult to pinpoint."

"Didn't Alice and Alfred want you?" Peg wondered.

"Oh yes, they did indeed," Rosie found herself answering. "Very much indeed."

Peg turned to Edna. "That doesn't make sense."

"We must keep to the questions. Now, Rosie. Imagine three thousand and nineteen tulips from Holland, which you have never seen. Now imagine a collection of twenty-eight copper saucepans. They all suddenly fall into a river in Britany. So what happens to all the fish?"

"There weren't any," Rosie said impatiently. "Your hypothesis is absurd, and fish are sensible little creatures, so they don't fit together. Your river is therefore a fantasy and fish do not swim in fantasies. Besides, I told you already, it's ninety-eight. And the fish would be singing ninety-eight over and over again."

"Very well," sighed Edna. "Multiply thirteen by a hundred and fifteen, then divide the answer by two and multiply again by seventy-seven. What's the answer?"

"Ninety-eight," Rosie said patiently.

"That seems accurate," said Peg, counting on three of her fingers.

"Repeat after me," Edna cut in, "Gold tassels."

"Pirates and pillars," said Rosie.

"Perfect," smiled Edna. "Now, repeat after me again. Bristles and badgers."

"Otters and ovens," Rosie murmured, "plus ninety-eight. You can subtract one from ninety-eight and still arrive at the answer ninety-eight, but the otters won't know how to put it in the oven."

"You're doing very well, my dear," Edna told her. "Only a few more questions, and it will be all over."

"I'm happy to carry on," Rosie smiled.

"Good," said Edna, her voice falling to a virtual whisper. "So tell me about the dark."

And Rosie began to explain.

CHAPTER TWENTY

S he was still under the spell when Rosie began to explain the shadow side,

"There are two systems by which darkness can inspire a wizard or witch," she said, her eyes still firmly closed as she relaxed in the chair. "Some wiccan folk are born dark. They are the evil ones and are not too difficult for another wiccan to recognise. But then there are those who have some magical power, but with little idea of what to do with it. They are simple, even kind, and invariably weak. A strong shadow can easily manipulate such a wizard. This is inclined to bring out the wizard's own light side, but deny it sustenance, so that the brain becomes detached. The result is simple, although it can take several months or even years to create the full result. Then the wizard is assumed, even by himself, to be kind but excessively stupid. On the other hand, the shadow can be triggered, and the simpleton should turn dark as the night. His brain returns, and he will search for actions to satisfy his desire for cruelty."

She paused and Peg asked, "Is that Boris Barnacle you describe?"

"It was," Rosie nodded. "But no longer, since the wizard is dead,"

Peg stared, and Edna asked, "In retaliation? Did he fight with someone who got the better of him?"

"No," said Rosie. "His death was planned."

"Who by?" Edna whispered.

"Alice, naturally," said Rosie.

Peg ran from the room and slithered down the stairs. Edna clapped loudly, bringing Rosie out of the trance, and taking her hand, flew with her down to the room normally occupied by Boris.

His door was open, and already Peg stood there in silent horror. Parts of Boris were scattered across the floor and huge streams of blood were running from one part to another, oozing between the floor boards and collecting around the head. The head itself, face down, was cracked and a number of black globules had leaked out. Where pieces of his body had been removed, it seemed not only unnecessary, but frenzied.

"The shadow side?" Edna whispered. "But clearly not of Boris himself."

"Alice," muttered Peg.

Which is when Alice strode from the kitchen and surveyed the stinking mess on the floor. With both arms upraised and hands fluttering, she began to scream. The echoing cry continued for some moments, and everybody from every room in The Rookery came running, flying or creeping to see what on earth had happened now.

"Oh, not again," sighed Montague.

"Well, this one won't be missed,' said Mandrake.

Nan Quake, who rarely left her bedroom in spite of her respectable seventy-five, stared down at the ghastly sight, and her scream joined Alice's. Inky and Julia both pushed through the growing crowd and stood in absolute disgust. Inky dropped the pair of shoes she had been holding and screamed too, although with a higher tone. Nan's scream was much deeper. Julia Frost simply burst into tears. Inky's shoes had landed in a pool of blood, and she refused to ever to wear them again.

Toby stepped backwards into Dandy, and both swore at each other. Harry Flash started crying as well, while Ethelred got the hiccups and hurried off.

In the middle of this, Rosie sat on the bottom step of the nearby stairs and tried to remember and make sense of what had been happening up in Edna's room. Edna herself leaned back against the wall without expression, while Peg rounded on Alice.

"It was you," she accused. "We know it was you."

"How dare you," Alice screeched. "Indeed, I know who it was. Not me, of course. This was Alfred. My wicked husband. I know it, he murdered them all. He was looking for something though I've no idea what that was."

"A silver cup?" suggested Peg.

Alice turned as red as the blood on the floor. "What nonsense. I'm telling you; Alfred did this. I've had to live separately from my husband for years since he was so vicious. I forced him to live as far away as possible, or I knew he might hurt our little Rosie. Indeed, have you seen what he did to her bedroom? He had some idea about precious objects he could sell, so he killed Whistle. Then Kate and now this. I am so frightened of him." She finished with a gulp, pointed at the pieces of Boris and returned to the scream.

One or two of the more sympathetic witches rallied around to comfort Alice, giving her a slight hug or two. Nothing really affectionate, since no one actually liked her.

Looking up at the still fussing crowd, Rosie said, "Not my father. It was him who came to me three nights ago. Poor darling, he can't fly, but he managed to scramble through my window to warn me I was in danger. He never said who from, but obviously it wasn't him or he would have killed me there and then. He helped me hide, and then he disappeared."

"There you are, then," Alice roared. 'He got rid of you – knowing exactly where you were, in case he wanted to come back and kill you off. But in the meantime, your room was unoccupied and ready for him to go in and search for valuables and take as long as he liked. Then he did the same to his own room, just to make him seem more innocent."

"Pooh," said Rosie. But she had no proper answer.

Edna answered for her. She pointed one very long finger, and everyone saw as a huge blue flash exploded from the end. "Tell the truth," she ordered. "Who killed Boris Barnacle?"

Alice went white. She swayed, but was unable to escape the spell. She gulped, croaked about a sore throat and then suddenly blurted out, "Me!" and shuddered. "But only this one," she shrieked. "Not Kate. Not Whistle. Those weren't me. I think they were him." She waved a cold hand at Boris's pieces. "That's why I killed him."

"Then why on earth say it was all my father?"

Alice stared around, wiped her nose on her apron and shouted out, "I have to go. Nearly time for supper." And she ran towards the kitchen.

Montague had wandered off, but Mandrake marched to the front door. "This is a job for the sheriff," he said, and slammed the door behind him.

"Oh, bother," said Peg.

"No matter," said Rosie, remembering Dickon Wald.

Rosie was asleep again when the sheriff's assistant arrived. Clearly he was quite pleased to be back and knocked politely on the front door even though it was open. Mandrake beckoned him inside and led him to the chaos in Boris Barnacle's bedchamber. With one brief glance, Dickon turned away, fisted his hands and shut his mouth with a snap. Clearly Dickon felt quite sick, and heaved, but managed to hold it in.

"No need to investigate the remains," Dickon said quickly with a gulp. "A nasty brutal death. Someone must have hated him indeed. Clearly male, clearly strongly built with a vile temper. Now, which of your residents would you say fits that picture?"

"None of them," said Mandrake. "Possibly the owner, who is definitely female."

"No, impossible, no delicate lady could do such a thing."

"I suppose you're not married," sighed Mandrake.

"I should like to speak with Mistress Rosie," Dickon, avoiding any view of the mess on the floor. "She'll be able to tell me everything I need to know."

Mandrake laughed. "I'll get her," he said, "but she's already accused her mother."

"Nonsense," declared Dickon. "I shall wait in your meeting hall." And, remembering where this was, he strode off in the opposite direction to Mandrake.

It was quite some time before Rosie joined him, and she looked glassy-eyed and still half asleep. "You want to know about Boris?" she asked.

"You must not, under any circumstances," Dickon told her, his hands on her shoulders in protective fashion, "go anywhere near Master Barnacle's bedchamber," and stared earnestly into her eyes. "You must not even go close. It is a crime of the worst sort. Now, my dear, if you'll forgive me for calling you that," and he led her to a couple of the more comfortable looking chairs, "who do you suppose is capable of such an evil and brutal murder?"

"My mother," said Rosie, retrieving her arm from Dickon's grasp.

"No, no," Dickon said, a little concerned. "I presume you've recently had an argument with your mother, and so you feel a little cross with her. But this is the ugly work of a malicious male. So can you help me with a possible culprit?"

Regarding him with little remaining sympathy, Rosie sighed. "I have no idea," she said. "We're all very nice people here. It must have been someone from the village."

"And have you any reason why this gentleman might have been killed? Was he wealthy?"

"Oh, yes," lied Rosie with a faint smile. "He had a large wooden chest full of coins. He's been collecting it for years, working so hard for that reason. If you find someone with a chest like that, then it's obviously the killer. But the chest might be rather hard to open."

"Locked, I assume," Dickon asked. "We should discuss the situation a little more fully, mistress. Would you care to come to the Juggler and Goat with me for a light meal and some ale? I'm sure it would be a great help to me."

"Umm," said Rosie again, "trouble is, I've promised to spend the evening with two friends here. Old ladies, you know, who get rather lonely. But I think you should do a search for the money chest. Perhaps start under my mother's bed."

"Dear, dear, you really have had a strong disagreement with your poor mother today," Dicken said, trying to reach for Rosie's hand again. "But I promise, no female, especially past a certain age, could ever have committed such a horrible act."

Pulling her hand away again, Rosie managed a smile, meanwhile wondering what on earth she had found attractive about him before. She decided that the attraction must have been for the tavern and not the man. "This isn't the first murder here," she said as he nodded. "So have you got any rough and greedy men wandering around in Little Piddleton? Or perhaps already in gaol? Or someone who used to be poor but has got suddenly rich?"

"Perhaps if you're not free today, then what about tomorrow at the tavern for a chat?" Dickon pressed.

"Maybe tomorrow. If you can think of possible killers in the village." He was thinking deeply as she stood. "Well, sorry, but I'm going back to my friends upstairs. Are you going to question everyone like you did last time? In that case, don't forget my mother."

Dickon stood as she did, pushing back his chair and clutching her hand. "Tomorrow at the Juggler and Goat, then. At five of the clock? May I come and collect you?"

"Oh, I suppose so," Rosie said, pulling away but relishing the thought of good ale and a sumptuous supper. "Good luck with the interviews."

Edna and Peg were waiting for her in Edna's pleasant second room, and Rosie flopped down beside them on a rather stiff little wooden chair. Edna patted her hand. "The sheriff's assistant is rather stupid, my dear, but that's a very good thing. It means we can all get on with our own lives without the law interfering. I have no idea what the actual sheriff is like."

"He sleeps a lot," said Peg.

"What a blessing." Edna turned to Rosie. "Now, you may remember what was going on before we were called down to see what was left of Boris. I do hope you realised what was going on."

Rosie remembered a dozen completely crazed questions, and her own completely crazed answers. "Then I remember you asking me about the shadow people," she said softly. "I know I said quite a lot, but you had me under a special spell, didn't you, because there's no way I actually knew any of that. But I said Boris was one of those very weak little wizards who got infected with shadows by someone horrible. The weak ones can't resist, can they? I was so scared for my father."

"No strong magic," Peg said, "but clearly he cares for you very much. That would save him from the shadows, even if nothing else could."

"But Boris didn't escape. And what about my mother?"

"Ah, yes." Both Edna and Peg leaned back in their more comfy and cushioned chairs and smiled, hands in their laps. "Your mother is clearly another split wiccan, just like Boris. Not quite as weak on the good side, and a good deal stronger on the darker. She must have been turned some years back, but not before you were born, because I cannot believe Whistle would have chosen her as your adopted mother if she was heavily shadowed. And he would have known, you know."

"The me under your spell," Rosie said, "was quite sure. She knew it was my mother."

"Your adopted mother."

Rosie was shaking her head as she tried to remember everything else. "The spell, and what you were doing, and those funny questions," she said, "that was all strangely familiar. But how can it be?"

"Quite simple, my dear," Edna said. "What you vaguely remember happened around fourteen years ago when you were tested. I was there, you see. I helped with the test. Whistle was also there, taking an interest, of course. We all expected a high score. But sadly, it came out only as a fifty. That puzzled us, but we had to accept what came up, or we would have been accused of cheating. But I have always wondered if someone blocked you, someone very strong indeed who might have put a spell – even a curse – on you as a very young child. That would have smothered your skills and made you appear far weaker."

With a blank stare, Rosie swallowed meekly, not understanding. "What on earth for?"

"That's the one thing we just don't know," said Peg. "And it must have been such a strong wizard, which doesn't really fit in with the rest of the story. But never mind about that. We know enough, for clearly your mother employed someone to do it for her."

Rosie didn't know why that would have happened either. "If she wanted me as a baby, why make me stupid?"

"That's something else we do know now," smiled Edna. "We know almost everything, since I had some information from Whistle a long, long time ago."

"And now I've been able to read a lot of Whistle's papers," nodded Peg.

"But in the meantime," Edna continued, "wouldn't you like to know what score you earned in the wizarding Wiccan Test?"

"Not really. Fifty-one, fifty-two? Even fifty-five? Not forty-five I hope, though I wouldn't be surprised."

"Oh, dear me no," said Edna. "You've scored ninety-eight."

CHAPTER TWENTY-ONE

Rosie's sigh was both anticipation and boredom. She was well aware accepting Dickon Wald's invitation had been absurd and even greedy. He was not a revolting person for a plain human, but like most humans, he spoke more nonsense than sense. However, she had grown to enjoy the food and atmosphere on offer at the Juggler and Goat, and after years of her mother's cooking, a mixture of magical manifestation along with genuine production, anything else was preferable. She also liked knowing what sort of official clues this sheriff's assistant might have discovered.

Rosie was therefore ready for Dickon when he turned up, and they walked together down Kettle Lane towards the village and its colourful tavern. As summer approached, the days had grown steadily longer, and now the sky was a huge blue blanket of warmth, although the bliss of blossom had long finished and blown away. Bluebells still followed the paths and banks, but the delicate froth of the lilac had hidden and dropped as new leaf crowded trees and bushes.

Feeding their young, the crows were more aggressive than usual and had no time for chats on the fence, and with no wish for interruptions that would be extremely difficult to explain to a human, Rosie walked more quickly than Dickon had expected.

"You must be hungry, Rosie, dear," he said. "Longing to get a cup of ale, perhaps?"

Trying not to sound scornful, Rosie nodded. "Thirsty – yes. And I thank you for the kind invitation. But you really shouldn't call me 'dear', you know."

"The second special meeting?" Dickon grabbed her hand and thrust it through the crook of his arm. "We are quite a little pair, you know."

Uncertain as to the practices of humans, Rosie accepted this but still pulled her hand away. "Business meetings," she insisted. "After these shocking murders, a discussion with an expert is simply sensible."

Clearly, Dickon was disappointed, but knew females had the reputation of saying 'no' when they meant 'yes', so he pushed open the tavern door, and pulled out a stool for Rosie to sit. From the peaceful twitter and sunny breezes outside, they had suddenly entered the raucous laughter and clank of cup to jug, the deep dark shadows and the reflections of candle flicker in the rich red wine.

The dark shadows reminded Rosie of her recent education in the shadow side of magic, and she shivered. More importantly she continued to ponder on the absolutely unbelievable number of ninety-eight that she had been given.

Knowing it as a mistake and utterly wrong, it did not bother her too much. But how had it come up, and what did such a ludicrous test reveal? Even accepting the test as the right way to judge a witch, it made no sense. If she had been suffocated of power when young, how could a crazy number like ninety-eight pop up?

"Dreaming, my dear?" asked Dickon, carrying over the two brimming cups of ale. "Now, I know you were quite fixed on the odd idea that your mother had been involved in some way with that last shocking death at your home, but I do trust by now you've realised that is unjust. As you know, I interviewed everyone at the residence, and I have come to a tentative conclusion. Would you like to know?"

Since he had chucked the whole idea of privacy, Rosie nodded immediately. "I need to know, to keep myself safe," she said with conspiratorial appreciation.

"Your gardener," smiled Dickon. "Quite obvious really. He's very large and wide-shouldered, he must be strong for the work he does, and he has many weapons at hand, such as a spade and an axe amongst others. I also gather he is paid almost nothing beyond his keep, so is bound to be somewhat sulky, of course, being the one working so hard for so little, when many of your inmates are wealthy folk who do nothing to help."

"I don't think anyone would commit such a brutal crime because of simple sulks," Rosie said. "Besides, I like Dipper. He's a nice and generous man. And it's true, he earns very little, but he only works when he feels like it and has his own room and food supplied. Kate, the maid who was killed, she lived next to him, and they were close friends."

"Ah," said Dickon, clearly thinking of himself, "but men often have an idea of what they'd like to do with a female friend, and if she says no, then he may get angry."

"Is that a warning?" Rosie blinked.

"What a shocking thought," said Dickon at once. "Certainly not. But—" and he watched her carefully over the brim of his cup, "I am certainly hoping that we can become better acquainted."

Luckily, the platters of food arrived at this moment, and Rosie was able to escape answering. Instead she hurried to fill her own platter with the three dishes on offer, drained her cup and concentrated, eyes down. Earlier that day she had already explained the situation to Peg, and there was a solid arrangement for Peg to turn up and save her. But Peg had not yet come.

As the thick sliced lamb's liver soaked in Burgundy and stuffed with smoked bacon, onions and a variety of herbs was quickly finished, and both Rosie and Dickon had started on the dried figs boiled in milk with sliced apple baked in pastry, Dickon abruptly leaned across the table and, gazing into her eyes, said, "Indeed, my dearest Rosie, I would like you to be my wife." His mouth was full so he was spitting apple juice as he spoke, but none of it reached Rosie as she had quickly pulled away, almost falling backwards off her stool.

Rosie hadn't meant it, but she knew that, somehow, she had caused it, when Dickon started coughing. The heaving, gargling cough was clearly uncontrollable, and with a splutter of misery he disappeared behind his sleeve as he continued to cough and then sneeze.

With a huge effort, which made Rosie feel guilty, Dickon closed his mouth, but his face puffed up and turned quite purple. Then as he stood, in the hope of clearing his chest, he found himself hopping. Desperate, but unable to stop, Dickon hopped around the small table, but when he tried to apologise, all that came out was another coughing fit. The hop then turned to a wild and energetic dance, and with a huge leap he started to kick and bounce, twirl and twist, encircling the entire width of the tavern.

Several of the folk sitting around began to clap and cheer, thinking it intentional, but in an agony of disbelieving embarrassment, Dickon rushed from the Juggler and Goat.

As he hopped out, Peg marched in. She sat on the stool Dickon had abandoned. "That will serve him right." she said, arranging her skirts and eyeing the remaining platter of food.

"Did you do that?" asked Rosie, half laughing.

"Goodness no," Peg told her. "You must have done it yourself, my dear. Your strengths are starting to reappear."

Amazed and somewhat horrified, Rosie stared. "It couldn't have been. I don't know how to do things like that, and I never intended it. Honestly, it wasn't me."

But Peg insisted. "This is how it happens," she said, "when someone has been under a suffocation spell for years. Your ninety-eight was squashed down to almost half. Now that full power is pushing its way through. I'm quite sure you'll have a lot of fun over the next year, finding out just what you're capable of."

Peg ate the rest of the fig and apple tart with loud appreciation and magicked up some cream to plop on top. As a final moment of pleasure, she ate the remaining quarter slice of liver and smiled widely. "Right, off home." And she paid the tavern owner, took Rosie's hand, and they left, closing the door behind them. Once out of sight, they flew back to The Rookery and straight through Edna's window.

"I doubt that silly young human will bother you again, my dear," smiled Edna. "Come and sit down with us."

"I feel a bit sorry for him," Rosie muttered, "but he decided poor old Dipper was the killer, and we don't want that." She took the cup of wine Edna offered and added, "has anything happened with mother? Has she – perhaps – run away?"

Twizzle, having escaped from her perch in the other room, proceeded to answer everyone with a continuous flap around the room until she finally settled on Edna's shoulder. She insisted, "Good day, mate. Mind the billabong." Edna took no notice.

Peg frowned, tapping her fingers on her knees. "No such luck. Your wretched mother is protesting her innocence. And no one here is sure what to do. After all, she owns this building, the grounds and almost everything in it. Everyone is nervous that if we press the guilty accusation, she'll burn it all down or produce a few trolls to threaten us or something like that. As a fifty, I doubt she's capable of trolls, but we can't be sure, and burning the place down could be too easy."

"I'm never going to do anything more for her," Rosie said, staring down sadly at her lap. "No beds or buckets of water. Besides, my bed's upside down. And I'll never call her Mamma again. But she did bring me up. I just feel so strange."

"Hardly surprising," Edna said. "But perhaps you are beginning to realise, my dear, that the terrible murders taking place here, actually have a great deal to do with you after all."

Rosie felt the slide of tears down her cheeks and bent her head further down. "Not really," she said. "None of it makes sense to me. And you two understand a lot more than I do, but you won't tell me."

"We know bits and pieces," nodded Peg. "But not how it all comes together. So even if I wanted to explain everything to you, I couldn't. And besides, a glorious ninety-eight should be able to explain it to me, not the other way around."

"I'm not a real ninety-eight," Rosie said a little sullenly. "You know I'm not."

"It's your potential, my dear," Edna cut in. "But first you have to thrust your way out of the fifty you've been living in. Only you can do that."

"Then perhaps, number one, I ought to fix up my bedroom instead of stealing yours," she answered. "And number two, I should talk to Dodger about where he found the silver cup and what else was there. And then number three, look for my father – I mean, Alfred – and make sure he's alright. Is there a number four?"

"Yes indeed," Peg replied. "Number four, relax and take your time. Everything will happen as is meant, and when it is right. Most of your learning will probably be slow, and not one single itsy bitsy is your fault, my dear."

The option of talking to the silver trio or even Oswald occurred to Rosie, but that made her feel strangely vulnerable, and in front of Peg and Edna, Rosie knew she'd be judged as a failing ninety-eight sinking down to the level of a fifty or less, so she stood, straightened her shoulders and said she'd start with number one. Rosie then trotted down the stairs with no attempt to fly, and opened the door to her old room. Outside the crows were calling, the babies had stopped squawking and the sun had sunk below the horizon. The gloaming turned the sky a luminous blue, and every tree was a black maze of branches.

Her room, however, was unchanged. So without much hope of compliance, Rosie raised both hands and said softly, "Totally true but totally new, turn back how you were – make it gleam, nice and clean."

Then Rosie watched with a delighted smile and the entire contents of her room tumbled back into their proper places with very little noise and not a single mistake. The bed covers arranged themselves in order and tucked themselves in. The window polished itself, and the floorboards blew away the dust. A very small pink mouse scurried out from under the ruin of her best tunic on the floor, apologised with a sniff of whiskers, and ran out of the window, interrupting the mullions' dutiful polishing. The gown itself gathered up all its torn pieces, managed a few twists and turns, put itself all back together with a little shake and hung itself on a hook. Other items of her clothing cleaned themselves to such an extent, Rosie knew they were cleaner than when she had last worn them. Even her second-best apron reappeared without the large splodge of candle wax which had previously been there, and the mud disappeared from her little black boots.

Gazing with pride and relief at her restored bedchamber, Rosie decided to add a few things. "Some paper, ink and pen," she said, clicking her fingers. "And with the quill, I'd like a very fancy feather." It was a peacock feather, and since she'd never seen a peacock, Rosie was most impressed.

"Now a very large Turkey rug almost over the whole floor." It appeared. Deep crimson and elaborately patterned, it was so thick, Rosie felt almost cushioned.

"And now," she added, her smile almost splitting her face, "a big squashy cushioned chair beside the table." Red, voluminous, as comfortable as a bed, Rosie sank down on the most comfortable chair she had ever known. So, incredibly grateful, she added, "And invite that mouse back again. He's perfectly welcome."

The mouse thanked her with sniffy gratitude and ran back under the bed.

Leaving her room with huge satisfaction, she even waved it goodbye, Rosie faced the stairs back up to the attic and Edna's rooms, and for the very first time in her life without someone holding her hand, she flew. It felt wonderfully exhilarating, and Rosie was so excited, she flew straight into the room where Edna sat, and almost bumped into her. Twizzle shot up and demanded a cup of Vegemite.

"Done," Rosie said. "I did it. I made it tidy itself. The bed flopped off the ceiling, and the table spun off the wall, and they all sorted themselves. Even my old clothes cleaned themselves and hung themselves up. And then – " she almost danced, "I created new things. "A wonderful chair. A gorgeous rug. Oh, Edna, dearest, I am truly discovering myself."

"I'm thrilled," Edna told her. "But not surprised. This is real power, my girl, and the power is all yours. Enjoy it. So come and sit down. We have other things to attend to."

"Why couldn't I do it before?" Everything was still one huge confused puzzle.

"Because, my dear, you had been suffocated. presumably by your mother, if she had the strength, or someone on her behalf. And you had no idea that you actually had more strength hidden beneath, so you never tried to rise above it. And," she grinned suddenly, "I've been knitting away to remove the suffocation cloud, stitch by stich."

Leaning over with excitement and delight, Rosie put her hands on Edna's shoulders and kissed her cheek. "What a wonderful darling you are," Rosie exclaimed. "And Peg too, of course. Where is she?"

And at that exact moment, the door was hurled open, and Peg rushed in, flapping three pieces of thick parchment. "I've found it," she said. "This will solve it all."

CHAPTER TWENTY-TWO

Now late, the night was closing in. But excitement ignored tiredness. They all three sat around the table again, where Peg laid out the three pieces of parchment. The pages were unmarked, and it seemed as though they contained nothing at all. But Peg began to whisper a spell, several times mentioning Whistle's name, and concluding with a hearty "Done."

The words began to appear. Edna leaned over eagerly to read them.

This is the document, officially verified by his highness Tulip Onceover, to state that the property in Kettle Lane, in the shire of Wiltshire, including all buildings thereupon, in particular that known as The Rookery and its out buildings, and the entire grounds, trees and other plants, including the well at the side of the property, are of one single occupancy and ownership, being that of Master Whistle Hobb, a proven ninety-one and three quarters.

As the sole owner since the year in human terms known as 1278, Master Whistle Hobb is entitled to do whatever he wishes with this property, except that of destruction. For this entire property has been originally built by one Spencer Ludgate Hobb, who has marked it with a damnation on any witch, wizard or human who attempts to ruin any part, including the trees, bushes and other plants.

Since this property was created for Mistress Flordal Bonnet Hobb, Whistle Hobb's mother, it is protected in her name on her sad demise.

Whistle Hobb is free to designate whomever he pleases as the inheritor of this estate, but the inheritance must be accompanied by some relationship, however small. If absolutely no person can claim a relationship, then the entire property must be passed over to the country for the use of aged and disabled souls, preferably of wiccan descent.

In the meantime, the rights of this estate belong solely to Master Whistle Hobb and if any harm is done to him, then the consequences shall be as follows:

Whomever has performed or ordered to be performed an act of aggression towards Whistle Hobb during his lifetime with any relevance to the ownership of this entire property, will be held in contempt of the Wiccan Court. If found guilty, they will be exploded on the spot.

This consequence is under the ruling of the court, but any offender who manages to escape this sentence, will be immediately transformed into a common troilus bug, wherever it is, and be condemned to live in this manner forever during the criminal's lifetime.

Meanwhile, should Master Whistle Hobb be annihilated, then the entire estate of The Rookery shall automatically belong to Whistle Hobb's designated descendent, unless that designated inheritance be that same personage as awarded to Master Whistle Hobb's proven killer.

In such a case, the estate will be legally presented to the shire under the conditions stated above.

I hereby authorise every word within this document as undeniable legal imperative, and sign herewith.

The signature was large and very black, with the name Humbugnas Triampanze. The name was known to all as the first and only wiccan Lord of Rule, a wizard with a full and extraordinary one hundred, who was still alive somewhere, probably in some place utterly unknown.

With huge grins which were becoming almost fixed, Rosie, Edna and Peg all linked hands and nodded at each other with the satisfaction of the over eighties, having achieved the extraordinary.

And with a twitch of absolute delight, Rosie said, "So it always belonged to Whistle. It never belonged to my adopted mother at any time."

"So why did he let her think so?" puzzled Peg. "Or was she somehow the designated relative?"

Rosie didn't need to think about it and quickly shook her head. "Impossible. Mother – I mean my adopted mother – didn't like dear Whistle, and I'm sure it was on her orders he was killed, even if she didn't do it herself, which she might have done. She's hardly a dainty little thing."

"It will be interesting to see if she turns into a bug, or gets flown off to the High Wiccan Court and exploded."

"It's been a few weeks," wondered Edna. "Whatever she deserves should have happened by now. Or perhaps," and she lit up in smiles again, "the court is sitting without her being present. In which case something deliciously nasty will suddenly happen to her out of the wild black nothingness."

"The sooner the better."

"I think," Rosie added, gaining confidence, "it's time we got the silver out again."

They lit two candles, then set up the toadstool, spoon and cup once more on the table, summoned a jug of cool clean water out of the air, and Rosie, this time with a hand as happily steady as a rock, filled each item with the water, and then drank. She felt the usual rush of exhilaration and a thread of burning excitement ran from her head to her toes.

"Where is Alfred Scaramouch?" Rosie asked, "and is he guilty of anything involved with these murders?"

After the prolonged taking and giving, and even though Rosie had squashed in two questions, the answer was clear. "He is in hiding with the owl known as Dodger." announced the cup. "And no, he is entirely innocent of every crime, except that of not trying to stop her when he realised she had wicked plans."

"Right," said Rosie, "Who murdered Whistle?"

"Boris Barnacle, on Alice Scaramouch's orders," was the expressionless answer.

"And who murdered Kate Cooper?"

"Boris Barnacle on the orders of Alice Scaramouch."

"And so who murdered Boris Barnacle?"

"Alice Scaramouch." No one was surprised at the answer.

"It's fairly clear at last," said Edna. "She had dear Whistle killed in order to take over The Rookery. And she ordered the killing of Kate, because she had stolen some of Whistle's belongings which Alice wanted. Then she killed Boris herself, otherwise he could have disclosed her orders, especially if he got caught himself. He was the only one who could know for sure."

"But what I don't understand," Rosie frowned, "is why Alice and Alfred claimed to own everything while Whistle was still alive, and he never denied it. He quite cheerfully let them take all the rents and all the favours and never spoke a word about himself."

"Ask the cup. Or ask your dear mother." Peg wagged a finger.

"The cup," Rosie answered, "is magic of a very superior quality. But none of them can explain things in death. It's all yes or no, or him or her, or some other very simple direction." She stood, smiling down at the others including the toadstool, spoon and cup just in case they felt insulted. "As for my darling mother – well – evidently I don't have one. So first thing tomorrow morning, I'm off to find my father."

Twizzle raised one foot, "No paddling in the billabong," he squawked, as Edna and Peg both wished Rosie goodnight.

After a twenty-four-year lifetime of feeling pathetic and no use for anything except cleaning up, Rosie jumped into bed, heard the strings creak beneath her mattress as they began to sing a faint lullaby and cuddled down to an extremely comfy sleep.

As planned, she woke before dawn, ready to achieve everything she desired.

Now able to fly wherever she wished, Rosie folded her skirts around her ankles and sped off towards the yew tree where she had been hiding only a few days past. She discovered the hole in the yew tree disappointingly empty of all but feathers, fluff, the occasional mouse and rat bone, and plenty of moss, twigs and old leaves. It actually smelled damp.

Clearly Dodger was no longer at home, even though this was the right time of day when he should have been fast asleep in his cave.

Aware that he had proclaimed a desire to live with Cabbage, even though she had thought he only meant for a night or two, Rosie flew back to The Rookery.

Flying on her own power came as a very different and remarkably pleasant experience. The wind blew through her hair, yet seemed quite friendly. The dawning sun waved good day. Rosie felt carried, as though sunshine, breezes, even rainbows, were all massing together to float her wherever she wished to go.

She certainly wished she'd been able to do this as a child as the experience would probably have seemed even more thrilling, and then, as she descended on the thatched roof, Rosie remembered doing exactly that. She had flown from the kitchen, where she was helping her mother, up to her father's tree house. But her father had trembled and told her this wasn't safe, and she shouldn't do it again. *"Oh no, my dearest darling Rosie, if she sees you, your mother will kill us both."*

When she had returned to the kitchen, Alice had greeted her with a great slap on the cheek, a punch to her nose, a kick to her stomach and had then grabbed her by the hair and swung her around the room almost dropping her in the fire.

"Don't you dare ever do such a thing again, monstrous brat," Alice had roared at her. "If I ever catch you flying again, I shall cut off your arms. Do you hear? And then the werewolves will come out of the forest and eat you all up."

Alice supposed Rosie had never dared try again, and surely whatever capability had then remained to her would have been blocked by the fear of such a threat.

Rosie decided that if Alice was ever turned into a bug, she would stamp on it.

Quickly finding the passage beneath the thatch into the small separate rood cavity, Rosie clambered and peered through the gloom to where Cabbage and Dodger were snuggled together in a flying fluff of lost feathers. They both awoke at her arrival, but neither seemed displeased.

"Oh, my dear Rosie," Dodger said, ruffling his neck feathers.

Cabbage, who was sitting looking in the opposite direction, simply turned her head right around. "Mistress Rosie," she said. "How sweet of you to visit."

"I'm sorry to wake you," Rosie said, although this wasn't true as she had fully intended to, "but I have a few extremely important questions." She sat cross-legged on the fluff and grinned at the two owls who now seemed about the same height as herself. "Could you please tell me," Rosie began very politely, since it was well known that being polite to owls was imperative, "where you actually found the silver cup you so kindly brought me when I shared your nest. Was it the last trunk under my mother's bed?"

"Indeed it was," Dodger told her.

"Thank you," said Rosie. "And would it please be possible, if not too boring for you, to explain what else was in that same chest?"

"Ah," Dodger said with a flick of one long ear, "I cannot promise that I noticed everything, mistress. The silver cup was on top, you see, and so I did not need to rummage. Certainly there were papers, being old parchment, for they lay beneath the cup. I am also quite positive I saw two other cups, one being red metal with a peculiar smell, and the other being copper, much larger, with impressions of flowers and letters engraved both out and in. The copper cup was truly beautiful, and I considered it surely made by a very talented engraver. However, the red cup, which sat in one corner within the chest, seemed somehow unpleasant. The smell was rancid, and I did not want it anywhere near my beak, so I was extremely glad you wanted the silver cup and not the red one. I am sorry I cannot remember any other item, for I doubt I saw any others."

A little bemused by the two other odd cups which had been described but she had certainly never seen, Rosie then asked, "And please, do you have any idea where Alfred Scaramouch is, who was always called my father, and used to live in the tree house out there? He was the one who brought me to your nest that night."

"Indeed I do," Dodger whooped owl-like. "That gentleman has been my friend for many years. Now being somewhat fearful of what may happen, he has taken up residence in the roof just next door. He frequently comes here for a bedtime discussion, and then sleeps the night here while we fly off to hunt. But when we return and wish to sleep, he goes next door and stays with the bats."

"Oh dear." Rosie wondered where she could hide him in a more comfortable and cleaner manner. "I'll go and see him," she said. "And thank you so very much for the information. You've been so helpful."

Returning to Edna's rooms, Rosie found both Peg and Edna dozing in their chairs, and so quietly tiptoed off downstairs to her own room, now so magnificently improved. Here, she wondered if she might doze too, but there was something else she wanted to do first.

Bending over her glorious new rug, she cupped her hands together and made up her own brand-new spell.

CHAPTER TWENTY-THREE

With her precious new creation cradled between her hands, Rosie flew quickly up to the roof cavity within the attic where the colony of small black bats were sleeping. They looked very peaceful, row upon row of little furry upside-down black objects hanging from the rafters. But beneath them was an extremely smelly carpet of guano, which covered the entire floor in various lumps of various sizes. Not quite as attractive as a Turkey rug

Alfred was cuddled in a corner with a slight slit of view through the thatch right beside him. He was entirely covered in guano and smelled no better than the rest of the space. He also appeared to be dozing.

Rosie crept to his side, tried not to breathe in the stink, and whispered, "Daddykins, it's me, Rosie. I'm quite sure the danger is past. Would you like to wake up?"

He woke gently with a flick of his eyes and a sweet smile. "I'd like to think the danger finished, my dear," he told her, voice little more than a grunt. "But sadly, not so, my dear."

"Well, Alice is still around," Rosie admitted. "But she can't do much, because there's the new resident Edna who is extremely powerful, and Peg too, who isn't exactly weak as you certainly know. And I've accused Alice of murder. She's denied it, of course, but she keeps very much out of the way, hoping it'll all blow over I expect. Boris is dead. He did the first two killings, didn't he?"

Her adopted father went red and looked very ashamed, saying only, "Umm."

"I know you know," Rosie explained. "But I honestly don't blame you. I bet you're frightened of Alice, just like the rest of us. Well – me, anyway. And you only knew because you couldn't help hearing it while she was plotting and planning. And you tried to save me – and it worked. I'm safe, and so are you. She thought she should kill me too, didn't she?"

Alfred nodded, still bright red amongst the shadows. "Umm," he managed.

"But she isn't my mother," Rosie continued. "And you're not my real father, though I've always loved you. So where did I come from, and why did Alice want to adopt me?"

"Oh dear," Alfred murmured. "I never understood half of it, you know. I knew it was Alice who wanted certain things and made them happen. I know a little about why. But we were only together for a very short time, you see. It was a love-spell, and I begged her to marry me. Silly old twit, I was. I should have guessed it was a trick. But she liked having a husband. I soon learned not to like her, but I liked being liked. Does that make sense?"

"Sort of. So when was I actually adopted? How old was I?"

"Such a sweet little baby," Alfred said with a smile that made his crimson flush disappear. "Tiny and quite adorable. A few weeks, perhaps. I'm not sure. Very young indeed."

With her own soppy smile, Rosie drank this in. Then she took a large breath to avoid the smell and asked, "Do you know anything about a large cup engraved with beautiful flowers and stuff? And maybe a small red cup that smells disgusting?"

This time Alfred shrank back. "I know nothing about the red cup," he said with an unconvincing shiver. "But the decorated cup is yours, my dear. Most beautiful, probably even valuable. Whistle Hobb presented it to you on the day of your adoption." His smile also seemed to be engraved. "You stretched out one tiny little plump hand, and touched the cup as he gave it to you. And he said, *'There you are – she accepts.'*"

"You liked Whistle? So what was he to me?"

Rosie had asked her ultimate question, but Alfred went suddenly quiet, The red flush reappeared. He muttered, "I don't know," and looked guilty. Rosie had already discovered that her adopted father was a very bad liar.

But she accepted his lie. As she now had other ways of finding out everything. So Rosie patted her father's arm. "I was hoping you'd come back down and take over Boris's room," she said. "I've made it clean itself up and those black splashes have gone. It's got a big hanging basket of lilac and bluebells and different sorts of blue flowers that don't exist here yet, but they won't ever die, and they all smell wonderful. I've put in new bed coverings and pillows, so none of them have anything to do with Boris, and they're all much nicer than his anyway, and there's certainly no blood left. His memory is completely gone from every tiny little scrap." Rosie watched his face for signs of dislike or worry, but Alfred appeared quite excited. "Of course, I'll clean up your tree house too," she promised him, "but since you can't fly or get your own nice food, I think you should use our nice big room downstairs most of the time. Perhaps you can go back to the tree for holidays."

"What a happy idea,' he said, scrambling to stand. "I thank you so much, my dear. You're very kind, even though now you know I'm not your real father."

"You've been my real father for twenty-four years," she smiled. "And that feels good enough." Rosie didn't add that since he had spent most of the time in the tree house, she hadn't seen him anyway.

But as she pulled something out of her apron pocket and held it out to him. He stared in wonder. He reached out, wiping one trembling finger over its surface. Rosie handed him her gift. It was a large ball of glass, and in its centre, imbedded but shining through, was a small glitter of silver stars.

"Is it what I think it is?" he breathed.

"Yes indeed. It's a Luck Glass," Rosie said. "You can ask lots of questions, and the answers show up in pictures. Sometimes it will even bring what you want. Ask for something important, and within three days you may get it. And just sit it by your bed, and it will bring a gentle mist of luck into your life, chasing away some of the bad luck that everyone gets. It won't do miracles, but it will do quite a lot. With the telling and the giving and the protecting, it will bring new feelings of safety and happiness into your life."

"That surely is a miracle." Alfred gazed lovingly both at the glass ball and at Rosie. "What a remarkable young woman you are, my dearest. And you are nearly of age now. Luck may come to you too."

But Rosie shook her head. "I'm only twenty-four, Daddykins," she reminded him. "It's almost another year before I turn twenty-five." And this time it was Alfred who shook his head.

"No, no, my dear. Has your mother told you wrong days and years for your birthdate all this time? Yes, I can guess she had a reason for that. But I have to tell you this, Rosie dearest, though I beg you not to tell your mother that it was me who told you. But your real birthday is at midnight, the sweet starlit witching hour, on the eighteenth of June. And this year, at midnight on that day this year, you will turn twenty-five, the moment when you become an adult wiccan and receive the blessing of the Great Lord of the Law."

The confusion fogged around Rosie once again. "Why on earth didn't Alice want me to know my real age? But for so many years she hid my powers too, and had me blocked. Suffocated. She wanted me as her daughter, but she wanted me weak and pathetic. It seems so daft. But then again, now I know she's such a terrible person, I suppose I'm not surprised at anything. And receiving my coming of age will be so wonderfully exciting."

"I am sure it will be glorious," Alfred said. "We are mostly hundreds of years old, so very few of us remember turning twenty-five. Your celebration will be a rare and delightful experience for all of us."

"Twenty-five. Ninety-eight. Twenty-five. Ninety-eight." Rosie repeated these important numbers to herself with pride. She held out her hand, grinning, since previously she had needed someone else's hand in order to fly herself. Now Alfred took her hand, and together they few down to Boris Barnacle's room, and Alfred stood gazing with enormous pleasure. It was now a grand room, and totally changed. So he rested his new Luck Ball on the little table beside his bed and flung his arms around his adopted daughter.

From Boris's room, Rosie walked directly to her adopted mother's. Few had seen Alice since the accusations, Boris's death and the day's interviews by Dickon Wald. Her scowl had occasionally been noticed in the kitchen, walking outside and even stalking the corridors. But she had produced neither breakfast nor dinner, neither supper nor any drinks and snacks. Indeed, she had almost disappeared. Rosie was sure the woman was planning something unpleasant, but still had no understanding of why.

Rosie saw no one as she entered Alice's grand bedchamber overlooking the garden at the back of the house. The ground floor, of course, since Alice was unable to fly. The room was empty, and immediately Rosie pulled out the last wooden chest hidden beneath the bed.

Having been already opened by Dodger, the lid sat a little ajar, and inside Rosie was able to see exactly what Dodger had described to her. She brought out the large decorated cup which she could not remember ever being given. As a valuable object, she assumed Alice had taken it for herself as soon as Whistle was out of view.

Rosie took the cup and put it into her apron pocket, where it hung heavy. She reached out to take the red cup, but pulled back her fingers, before touching, for a sudden spike of scarlet fire sprang from its centre, and the smoke was black and fierce. Even without touching, her fingers felt burned, and the stench curled upwards, crawling into her face, her mouth and her nose.

At once, Rosie ran to the well outside, leaving the bedchamber door open. Pulling up one bucket of water, she ducked in her entire head, clearing her sight and taste.

Slowly emerging, her hair dripping and water rolling from her face, she turned, and stopped.

"Frightened, my dear daughter?" said Alice.

Rosie wasn't sure what to do. Against a fifty, she now knew she could protect herself, but there was some dark power resident in that cup, and it had befriended Alice. Whether that brought their power to an even force, Rosie didn't know. The other power might be still greater than her own. Raising her chin, Rosie faced the other woman and laughed.

"Do you expect me to kill you? I've no desire to do that. But I shall take you to court for fraternising with the shadow side, and for the murder of three wiccan folk, including the great wizard Whistle."

"Take me to court? I'd like to see you try." Alice was fiddling in her own apron pocket.

There was no overpowering stink, therefore Rosie guessed she had a knife and not the red cup, so continued to smile. "They'll come for you, once I denounce you formally, you know. The court officials will come to fly you off for trial."

"They can't touch me," Alice growled. "I have protection of another sort. You can't imagine my strength. I'll not be dying any time soon, wretched girl. It's you in danger. I should have killed you long ago, but I needed Whistle dead first. Now you'll be joining him."

Alice grabbed the long carving knife from her dirty apron pocket and rushed at Rosie. She raised and then swung the blade, but Rosie simply raised one finger and called, "Be still."

Alice seemed paralysed, her arm high, her hand clutching the knife handle, and her face contorted in hatred and anger. But nothing quivered, nothing changed. She remained unmoving. And as they stood there facing each other, there was a swoop of black feathers, and a large crow hurtled down and grabbed the knife from Alice's hand.

"Shall I drop it down the well?" cackled Wolfy.

"You're the best crow in the world," Rosie laughed. "Throw it back through the kitchen window. And my love to Wobbles and Cuddles and all the babies."

"They're growing up a bit now," Wolfy said. "But feeding them is so exhausting. I'm looking forward to the day when they finally learn to feed themselves."

"Well, here's a thank you," Rosie called – and clicked her fingers. A short distance from Rosie's feet, a pile of food suddenly appeared, scattering itself across the grass. Make-believe worms and beetles, small buzzing flies obligingly sitting there waiting to be eaten, pieces of bread torn into long crusts, gulps of cheese, and a few other small wriggling things that didn't actually exist.

"Quick," Rosie pointed. "All the other crows will be grabbing this as soon as they see it. There must be at least a hundred funny little baby crows around here, all squawking with hunger."

As Wolfy grabbed a huge beak full, Rosie turned back to Alice, releasing her from the spell. But as Alice jerked once more into action, Rosie again pointed a finger at her and shouted, "You will obey me. Listen carefully and obey. You will enter your bedroom where you will find one of your hidden chests pulled out from under the bed, and its lid wide open. Beneath the red cup of some evil power which you keep there, is a document signed by Whistle Hobb. You will bring it to me. You will not bring the red cup."

It was only after giving the order that Rosie wondered if she had done something remarkably stupid. She wanted the document, and she hadn't wanted to touch the vile thing lying on top. Her solution had seemed perfect. But she had known her own power for an extremely limited time and had not yet learned every way to use it. Alice had walked off in a daze, rigid and obedient. But once she herself touched the red cup, Rosie wondered if Alice would change.

She moved away, ready to fly back to Edna if it became necessary. Then she saw the truth of it.

From Alice's bedroom, a great black flame exploded outwards. For one brief blink, Rosie wondered if this was the high court's form of execution. Perhaps they had telepathically heard the truth of Alice Scaramouch and immediately passed sentence. But within one more blink Rosie realised the opposite. The black flame grew vast and swept across the garden towards Rosie.

The flame halted, flickering as though frightened. Its tip curled in upon itself as though licking its own wounds. Then Rosie turned and understood.

Every single resident of The Rookery stood grouped behind her. Legs apart, expressions determined, some with wands pointing at the flame and at Alice, others with their hands up and facing outwards to block whatever came next. In front and directly behind Rosie, Edna stood tall, and Peg stood short, and both of them pointed to Alice, small golden flames rushing from their fingertips.

"We've called the High Lord," Edna yelled at Rosie. "The power will be with us just long enough for them to find her guilty."

The black flame had hurt her, and Rosie knew herself injured, but her power remained, and she flung out one arm, and with the tingle of the immense power all around, the black flame disappeared in a sprinkle of dark ash, and Alice fell. She tumbled to the grass, first screaming threats and then screaming for mercy. Every part of her head and body began to vibrate, and clearly she was in pain. The croaks and yelps were at first piteous, and having thought of Alice as her mother for twenty-four years, Rosie had a moment's sympathy. But she did not move and said nothing. She simply watched.

Slowly Alice diminished. Her back shrank until she was forced to bend over onto her suddenly distorted hands and feet now tiny and wrinkled, inching into the ground. Her shoulders popped and became glued to her back, her legs turned to minute sticks, and her entire existence was blushed into a ragged brown, muddy colour which would disguise her entirely as she crawled and hunted. Last to change was her head. It shrank slowly, and with it her expression concentrated into narrow invisibility. For a moment she cried, but soon all the sounds had gone, and on the grass sat a tiny and extremely ugly insect, a troilus, one of the most insignificant but unpleasant insects in the country.

"The court," said Rosie, "has passed sentence."

CHAPTER TWENTY-FOUR

Lying crumpled and damp on the grass where Alice had stood, was the document she had been ordered to bring. Rosie bent and picked it up. There was no lingering smell of wickedness nor any wisps of unpleasant smoke, but she made no attempt to read it and handed it to Peg.

"It's Whistle's writing," she said, breathless. "But I don't think I can read it."

Peg took it eagerly and bent over, her nose almost to the page. Edna meanwhile turned to Dipper, who stood behind her. "The sad corpse lies out under the trees, but Boris must be buried as the others," she said. "There is also a highly unpleasant cup which I want buried deeply beneath him. None of us wish to touch that cup, so once the grave pit is dug, I shall summon that vile thing and order it to drop itself in. Then you can pile Boris on top. But first, we have some things to rejoice, and probably something to listen to afterwards."

Rosie stood just a little apart. She smiled at the crowd in front of her. Twenty-three witches and wizards stood there smiling back, including Dipper, carrying a spade, and Alfred with Dodger sitting on one shoulder, and Cabbage perched on his arm. There was Edna and Peg, peering over the badly creased document, trying to read what had been written there so long ago. There was Emmeline and next to her stood Ermengarde. Dandy Duckett was trying to stick his wand back into the opening of his doublet, and Toby Tucklberry was hopping up and down trying to see where Alice had gone.

Ethelred Brown was attempting to summon a cup of ale but couldn't manage it, and had to ask someone else. Obligingly Vernon Pike produced a large tankard full of strong beer and Ethelred wandered off. Nan Quake and Uta Hampton were gossiping together, and Julia Frost was telling Gorgeous Leek to stop being so timid just because she was only a dismal nineteen, and to remember what a fantastic result she had just achieved.

Mandrake marched around the whole group shaking hands, and Lemony Limehouse sidled over to Percy Rotten and asked if he'd like a walk in the sun. Berty Cackle stood on his own wondering whether he should find the Alice beetle and stamp on it, while Montague looked around vaguely, saying, "Isn't that the funny little girl that sweeps the stairs? Why doesn't her mother take her in hand?"

Harry Flash was jumping up and down in excitement, while Inky Jefferson, Butterfield Short and Pixie West went hand in hand to congratulate Rosie for finally getting rid of her mother.

Rosie thanked them but tried to explain that it hadn't been quite like that, when she was interrupted by Edna.

Holding up the sheets of creased but fluttering document, Edna spoke loudly, addressing everyone. "You will be interested to know a few things," she announced. "Personally, I don't care what any of you choose to believe, but here, at last, is the truth.

"Nearly twenty-five years ago, Whistle Hobb found himself, let's say for convenience, with a new born daughter, a child of tremendous potential. But he was a busy man with a constant stream of things he wished to do, and had very little time or patience. He rightly decided he could not possibly take on a baby to look after, and eventually, deciding the child needed both a mother and a father, that she must go to a married couple. He could not envisage giving the child to any ludicrous humans, but amongst the wiccan folk, there are few couples either married or living as a pair.

"But here, in The Rookery, one pair existed. A lowly but quiet couple, Alice and Alfred seemed the perfect answer. Whistle asked them if they would care to adopt the little girl, yet they apologetically declined. They knew nothing about babies and didn't want such a strong one, who would surely swamp them. So Whistle thought of a plan.

"At the time he was, and always had been, the sole owner of this entire property, the buildings, the forests, the gardens and almost the whole of Kettle Lane. Whistle had inherited it. He was, of course, a rich man. But he offered Alice and Alfred a term of twenty-four years and eleven months to take over the ownership entirely, and all the funds, payments and profits paid by the residents during this time, on the strict understanding and legal agreement that when his child reached her coming of age at twenty-five, she would inherit the property herself. Indeed, he states that should he die before that day, she should inherit immediately as long as she was over the age of fifteen.

"Well, we know that did not happen, for it was Alice who murdered Whistle, sending Boris to kill him so that she might keep The Rookery with no one knowing that she was not the legal owner.

"Simple as that. She wanted to keep it all for herself, and had made, and probably also cheated, a great deal of wealth from the temporary ownership."

Peg was losing her voice with all the shouting, but with a few croaks and gulps, she managed to finish. "Whistle and Alice made the agreement, and it was signed in court, but kept secret. None of us knew. But it is all here in several documents.

"Naturally over the years as Alice realised what she was about to lose, she made horrible plans, and also received help from a dark shadow. That is something we must certainly destroy. In the meantime, our High Wiccan Court has passed judgement, found Alice guilty on all counts, and turned her into a very small beetle. She'll stay that way until someone treads on her. And that might be me, if I see her. Or perhaps a crow will eat her and then probably feel sick."

A magnificent barrage of cheering and clapping followed this announcement, congratulations called to Rosie, Peg and Edna, and everybody hugging everybody else.

"So now The Rookery belongs to you, my dear?"

Rosie had barely absorbed the facts herself, but in the midst of the turmoil and chaotic happiness, Edna grabbed Rosie's hand, and they flew back up to Edna's rooms. Peg was beside them, and they all arrived with a puff and a gasp, sitting back at the little table with the silver toadstool, the spoon, the cup and a jug of water.

Twizzle said, "About time too," and snatched the chair away with her beak just as Peg was about to sit down. Twizzle cackled, and Peg looked up with a threatening glance.

"If you don't behave yourself," she muttered, "I shall turn you into a sand fly and send you off to the Gobi Desert."

"Do you have Oswald with you?" enquired Edna of Rosie as she helped Peg up off the floor. Gradually they settled, and Peg called for a cup of best wine each and a very large one for herself.

At first Rosie couldn't remember what Oswald was. Her mind was once again in a whirl. The adoption made sense, and she knew her adopted mother's character well enough to understand how the whole situation had happened. She had never known that Whistle was the original owner of The Rookery until recently, but then very few others had known either. They had only settled into the house as they felt their age slowing them.

But there was one thing she did not understand. "So Whistle was my father? I must say, he didn't take much notice of me, considering I was his child, but I suppose that was the whole point of the adoption.

Maybe he even thought that all that bad treatment from Alice would be good training for me. And the blockage and suffocation of my magical power, well, either he thought I was weaker than he'd thought, or he knew I'd get all my force back when I came of age."

"Yes, yes, all very correct and logical, dear," said Edna. "But you haven't answered my question. Are you wearing Oswald?"

"And," Rosie mumbled frantically, "clearly Alice wasn't that bad in the beginning. It was all the temptation and rising greed that got to her and changed her. But what I have to know, is who is my real mother?"

"Perhaps," sighed Edna, "I had better repeat my question once more, dear. Are you still wearing Oswald?"

"Oh." She tapped the ruby hat pin clasped just below her chin on the collar of her tunic. "Yes. He's here, probably listening to everything."

"You were given Oswald when you were whisked off into never, never land," Peg reminded her. "You lost all the other hat pins, but this most precious one stayed with you. Now I know why. Would you hand him over for a moment, my dear?"

Quickly she did as asked. Unclipping Oswald, Rosie gave him an affectionate little rub and passed the hat pin to Edna.

Edna did not hold onto the ruby pin but immediately laid it on the table in front of herself. "Now," she said, settling back. "You may wish to ask various things afterwards, which is why I have your obliging silver trio sitting here patiently ready. But I am going to tell you a story first, and then Oswald will join in. I'm afraid some of this will sound distinctly odd and probably quite unbelievable, but I just hope you will not be upset. I am going to tell you who you are.

"Whistle owned The Rookery and everything that goes with it for many long years. He rented it out to the elderly wizards and witches who wished a calm life, and he employed a very good wiccan cook and three maids. The place was beautifully run, but he himself took very little notice of what went on here. I wasn't staying here myself back then, but I was Whistle's far off friend.

"A brilliant wizard as I'm sure you always knew. A ninety-one, more or less, probably higher. And one day he decided to do the impossible. He summoned all his might and all his skills and a nice collection of feathers and down, water from the well and from the skies when it rained, small blossoms, flowers and growing plants, and mixed these all up with his endless spells.

"I came over several times to help him, and once I brought my own little kitten, very fluffy and white. On request, I left her with Whistle. He carried on with his spells, adding various things when he found them, such as fluff from a duckling, a couple of butterfly wings, a few drops of ink, a crow's feather and down donated by Cabbage, briar rose petals and rippled bubbles from a stream. Whistle went out often with his basin of precious objects, especially during the full moon, and sat in various parts of the grounds and the forest, singing to himself and stirring the mixture. When autumn came and he still hadn't finished, he added leaves of all kinds and all colours, sedge and moss.

"And then one night he went out again. There was a full moon, but there was also a dreadful storm with forked lightning. He made sure that the lightning did not strike directly into his basin. But it still wasn't enough and didn't produce exactly what he wanted. He added snow during the winter, then mushrooms and berries, the roots of many tiny plants due to grow in the following spring, and he went on adding feathers, fluff and spells of all kinds.

"He was becoming somewhat impatient, having worked a whole year on his experiment. But he refused to give up. Eventually as the weather improved in June, he believed he must now succeed. He felt he needed just one more thunderous storm, and this time he would encourage the sparks to dive straight into the basin. The storm arrived, crashing from light to dark and from silence to thunder. Whistle waited, holding the bowl high and hoping for the final spark. It took a long time in coming. Several times he wandered home with no result. But he never lost his trust. He was, after all, a ninety-one.

"Yet one June night, the eighteenth of the month, close to midnight as the full moon gleamed polished silver above him, the rain began to pour. I was again visiting him with my beautiful kitten, so was with Whistle when he once again marched out into the garden. He allowed just a little rain to fall into the basin, which he set down on the ground, hoping for lightning. He heard the thunder rolling far off and crossed his fingers, shouting loudly through his strongest spell. But as he called, he only realised at the very final moment, that my little kitten Rosie had leapt into the basin on top of all the damp mush already there at the bottom.

"And immediately there came the lightening, striking directly into Rosie's mouth and eyes. She looked up with a cheerful miaow and disappeared. I was horrified and began to cry, thinking my beloved kitten had been struck dead. There instead was a perfectly formed little girl baby with huge blue eyes and soft white hair. The baby chuckled and made one small miaow. Whistle was satisfied at last, and so was I. I stopped crying and gazed down at the baby as the rain stopped, and the storm rolled away."

"And that's how he made himself my father?" Rosie stared, open mouthed.

Edna and Peg nodded.

"So I'm actually a kitten" Rosie whispered.

"In a way," admitted Edna. "Which is why Whistle called you Rosie as well. And it's also why, knowing that your coming of age was getting very close, I came back here to live, to meet you and to find out how everything was going."

"Do you mind, dear?" asked Peg. "I suppose it's a little strange to discover you're actually your father's greatest experiment."

It was extremely hard to assimilate, but now Rosie was the owner of a magnificent and wealthy property, she was a ninety-eight in magical powers, and her only enemy had been turned into a beetle. She was free, rich and could do whatever she wished. She was sorry to have lost Whistle, but he wasn't her father in the normal way.

But then she looked up. Climbing from the ruby head of Oswald, was a wispy shape, quite translucent but both clearly visible and recognisable.

Rosie grinned. "Daddykins."

"My dear daughter, I've been waiting for this moment," Whistle said in a faint crackle as if coming from a great distance through a magical loud speaker. "How do you feel now that you know it all?"

"Miaow," said Rosie.

I do hope you've enjoyed Rosie's first adventure, there's lot's more to come in the following books so do have a look.

In the meantime, I'd love to hear your thoughts, so please leave a review for others to see.

I look forward to seeing you in the next in the series, The Piddleton Curse.

ABOUT THE AUTHOR

My passion is for late English medieval history though I also have a love of fantasy and the wild freedom of the imagination, greatest loves are the beauty of the written word, and the utter fascination of good characterisation. Bringing my characters to life is my principal aim.

For more information on this and other books, or to subscribe for updates, new releases and free downloads, please visit barbaragaskelldenvil.com

Printed in Great Britain
by Amazon

26279394R00108